DEDICATION

For BookTok, my most ardent and faithful lovers ... oh and to Devendra Banhart, who apparently likes this kind of thing.

-L.

ACKNOWLEDGMENTS

Some of these stories appeared separately in other locations online or offline, at the Storm Crow Manor's vending machine and other illustrious but unusual publishing venues.

Dino Stud

Lola Faust

Up close, the *Tyrannosaur*'s breath was even worse than Tallulah had imagined it could be: a charnel-house blast of decaying meat.

Instinctively she recoiled, scrambling back on hands and knees into the shelter of the shipping container, trying to hide from the monstrous reptile as it pushed its muzzle in through the door. As of yet, it seemed not hungry so much as curious about this tiny female intruder into its domain.

Huddled against the rear metal wall, heart hammering, Tallulah stared out at the glittering eye of the giant saurian as it peered in at her. Maybe if she stayed completely still, it would just go away. If she could only control her terrified trembling…

The creature opened its jaws and bellowed. Inside the container the sound was deafening, obliterating. Tallulah covered her ears and screamed.

Was this how it was going to end? Devoured by a dinosaur? Her mind flashed to the chain of events that had led her to this lethal impasse. She really had put herself in this situation for a man.

But not just any man. Reid.

And worse: given the chance to do it over, she knew she'd do the same thing.

Her fugue was interrupted by a vertiginous heave as the dinosaur worked its tail underneath the container, tilting it forward.

And then sudden vertigo, as the enraged beast picked up the container with its powerful arms, tilting it further.

Tallulah felt herself begin to slide towards the opening, towards the waiting jaws that would crush her, the sharp yellow teeth that would tear her to pieces.

She didn't even have the breath to let out another shriek...

CHAPTER 1

Tallulah finally found the Ranch on her fifth day in Independence, Missouri, after four days of odd glances and raised eyebrows when she asked where it was.

The waitress at Denny's had giggled as soon as she'd heard the name. "Oh, *that* place. Not sure you really want to go there. Those folks are…" She trailed off as she plunked a plate of eggs and whole-wheat toast down in front of Tallulah. "I'm sure they're lovely people. Just keep to themselves. Coffee?"

"Sure," said Tallulah. "What do you mean, they keep to themselves?"

"We just don't see 'em much," said the waitress. Her broad grin was friendly, and her eyes were sharp. "Not for years, in fact. Are you planning to stay long? I think my landlord's got a vacancy coming up at the beginning of the month. Nice little apartment. It's in town."

"Thanks. I'm just here for the summer, but I'll keep it in mind."

"You do that, darlin'. I'll keep an eye out for you."

The next day, at the post office, the clerk had a similar reaction when she asked about the Dino Ranch while buying stamps. "I don't know much about those folks," he'd said, as she was rifling through her handbag to find her wallet. "They don't come into town. Not for a very long time."

"How do they get supplies, do you think?"

The clerk snorted. "Oh, they're *dino* people. They probably have their own special mail-order stores. I don't think they need to follow the same rules as the rest of us."

"Maybe they just get Amazon deliveries."

"Maybe." The clerk fixed Tallulah's eyes with his. He was an older man, sixtyish, with thinning hair and a round face; like the waitress, his eyes were sharp and watchful. "Either way, I don't know that a girl like you needs to get mixed up with folks like that."

Tallulah thanked him, stuffed the stamps in her bag, and headed out into the sunshine.

It was a late-May afternoon. Schoolchildren ran down the sidewalk with their backpacks hanging from one shoulder, shouting and clamoring for after-school treats from their weary-looking parents. Sunlight glinted dustily off the hoods of ten-year-old Chevys and Chryslers. A few cyclists in spandex and bike helmets, obvious work-from-home urban transplants, rested at an intersection and reached into their panniers for snacks.

All the hustle and bustle of a reasonably prosperous small town in farm country.

There was no sign that this was the closest town to the most innovative, and the most dangerous, dino-breeding facility this side of the Mississippi.

Tallulah had read about the Ranch in a travel guide to the area that she'd found deep in the Buzzfeed archives. "The 18 Weirdest Places in Missouri": the Ranch was number seventeen.

"By now we're all so used to the Jurassic Park-ification of our daily lives that a dinosaur ranch seems almost commonplace," the article said. "But this one is different. It's called 'the Ranch'; like Madonna or Lizzo, it needs only one name. The dinosaurs' keepers insist on a 'barn-free lifestyle on hundreds of acres.' It's the closest you'll ever be to the true American West, but instead of buffalo and cowboys, you'll see a greater variety of dinosaurs than any other independent ranch in the state – and the only *T. rex* hatchery in the entire country, other than Dinosys in NYC and Beecee in Arizona."

When she showed it to her parents, they were naturally concerned. "That just doesn't seem safe," her father had said. "A *T. rex* hatchery? Have you ever seen one of those things in person?"

"Obviously not," said Tallulah. "No one has. Almost. But I'm a *paleontology student*, Dad."

"Yes, and when you first chose that path, there was no such thing as a living *T. rex*."

"That's why it's so cool!" cried Talluah. "I went to school to study dinosaurs, and when I started, all you could study was bones. And now, five years later, I can study real live dinosaurs. Who gets to do that?! Whose academic field ever changes that much?"

"I'll tell you what," called Tallulah's mother from the kitchen, "at least we know Lulu won't ever be unemployed."

"Small favors," grumbled her father. "Doesn't do much good to be employed if you're going to be eaten by a *T. rex* ."

"I'm not going to be eaten by a *T. rex* ," sighed Tallulah. "They've got safety protocols at these places."

"Have you even talked to these Ranch people?" asked her father.

"Not yet," Tallulah admitted. "They don't have a website or a phone number or anything. I'm just going to find out where it is and show up."

"So you don't have a job there yet. There's still time to cancel your trip."

"Wasn't it you who always told me to just show up, because that's more than 95% of people ever do?" Tallulah asked, more calmly than she felt.

"You did say that," Tallulah's mother called from the kitchen.

"I am twenty-five years old. I am a PhD candidate at the University of Missouri. I am a grown woman and I am going to show up at "the Ranch" and demonstrate to them that I can be a valuable asset for the summer. I don't need email. I'm going to do this the old-fashioned way."

Tallulah's father leaned back in his recliner and studied his daughter, standing before him in the sun-filled living room of the St. Louis house they'd lived in since before she was born.

He'd always been impressed at how much determination fit into her pint-sized body, ever since she was a child; she'd always been full to bursting with willfulness. It had been a mighty project to help her direct that powerful will into a drive to succeed. And now, he realized ruefully, he was seeing the end result: a young woman who knew what she wanted and would not give up until she had it.

"Alright, then," he said. "You've got my blessing."

"Thanks, Dad," Tallulah said with a smile. "That means a lot. But you know I would have done it either way."

"I know, Chicken," he said, rising from his recliner. He wrapped her in a bear hug just like he had when she was a child, using her childhood nickname. "That's why I love ya."

Now, in the bedroom of the Airbnb apartment she'd rented for two weeks, she was writing a postcard to her parents.

Did you know that chickens and other birds are descended from dinosaurs? They're theropods, like T. rex. Just smaller. And did you know that Independence is where Mormons believe the Garden of Eden was? There are so many little signs that this is the right path for me. Or, if not

THE right path, at least it's some kind of right path. I'm going to learn so much this summer at the Ranch. I'll have conference presentations for years! Love you both.

Thought I'd send this the old-fashioned way, because there's nothing like getting real mail.

Your Tallulah.

She drew a tiny stick-figure chicken next to her name, affixed a stamp, and headed back out to the post office to drop it in the mailbox. It was only a fifteen-minute walk through Independence's old downtown. There were a few boarded-up storefronts along with little local businesses, and a few number of chain stores: Dollar Tree, Walgreens, the standard fast-food joints. But despite these encroachments of modernity, and despite Independence's proximity to Kansas City right next door, she felt its small-town-ness like a bright spot, like a beacon. There was something here for her, she was sure of it.

Something close by, anyhow.

"Hey!" shouted someone from behind her, just as she reached the post office.

Tallulah spun, long brown hair whirling around her face. A tall, freckled teenage boy in basketball shorts and a baggy T-shirt was jogging towards her. "I think you dropped this," he said breathlessly, holding out the postcard.

"Oh, my gosh," Tallulah groaned. "How did I manage that? Thanks so much."

The boy stopped and glanced down at the postcard. "You're welcome, uh, Tallulah. Wait a second. You're going to the Ranch?"

Tallulah held out her hand. "It's not polite to read other people's mail."

"In my defense, this is a postcard," said the boy with a half-smile.

"Fair enough. Give it."

The boy handed it over. "Are you really

going to the Ranch? I don't think people are supposed to go there anymore."

"Why?" Tallulah asked.

He shifted uncomfortably. "I don't rightly know, exactly. We just aren't supposed to go there. I think something happened with the lab."

"Where's 'there'? Can you at least tell me where the Ranch is?"

"Out Norborne way, if I recall," said the boy. "My brother went there for a field trip once. But that was years ago. No one really talks about the Ranch anymore."

"Norborne," said Tallulah. "Thank you so much… what's your name?"

"I'm Connor," said the boy. "Hey, can I ask you a favor?"

"What's that?"

"Please don't talk to anyone else about the Ranch, ok? It's just one of those things. People get nervous. It's not good."

Tallulah nodded, suddenly self-conscious. "Got it. Thanks, buddy."

As Connor ran off ahead, Tallulah's mind was racing with anxiety… and excitement. All the local secrecy around the Ranch only made it more enthralling for her. What mysteries could possibly be hiding out there?

What paleontological wonders would she discover, once she found it?

It could make her career. It could make her *life*.

She dropped the postcard into the mailbox and headed straight back to her Airbnb. *Norborne way*, she thought. *See you tomorrow, Ranch.*

CHAPTER 2

I'm really glad I filled up on wiper fluid, thought Tallulah, less than an hour into her journey. The windshield of her little blue Kia seemed perpetually covered with a fine brown dust that blew across the highway from the fields on either side, despite rows and rows of sprouting green crops. The sun shone down hard and bright. Tallulah donned her darkest pair of sunglasses and put on the "Summer Sunshine" playlist she'd been carefully building for this trip.

There was no way she'd let anyone, or anything, get her down. She was on her way to the Ranch.

She hadn't quite known how to dress for this… ambush. Field khakis? A professional pencil skirt and blouse? She'd ended up settling on something in between: wide-leg khaki pants with a crisp button-down shirt tucked in, her brown hair pulled back into a sleek ponytail that hung halfway down her back, and just enough makeup to look awake and eager: a swipe of black mascara to frame her green eyes, a bit of gloss to enliven her lips. She knew she often looked younger than her age, being as short as she was, but her fieldwork had filled her out and given her a solid, strong build. No one would ever call her *slight* anymore, and she loved it. She wanted to look like the kind of woman who would be able to do anything asked of her.

A woman who was suitable for physical pursuits.

And then, so rickety and faded that she almost missed it, there was the sign for Norborne, Missouri. It seemed almost an afterthought along the highway, with its peeling paint and weathered wood, as if the town couldn't quite believe that anyone would want to know where it was.

The night before she'd set off, at her Airbnb, Tallulah had spent some time with the Google Maps aerial view. She'd searched every building, every landmark, every field within ten miles of Norborne to find any evidence of Dino Ranch, since it wasn't marked on the map. She knew that farm country was characterized by wide open spaces – as the Dixie Chicks merrily sang on her "Summer Sunshine" playlist – but she'd grown up in St. Louis, and her city-girl heart was still astounded at the sheer number of falling-down barns and fallow fields.

And then she spotted it: a hulking shape in a copse of trees by the edge of a pond. She switched to street view to confirm her sighting, hoping against hope that the car-mounted camera had been powerful enough to capture what she thought it was, that the angle was right.

It was. The thing was barely visible, and it seemed to be hiding in the shadow of a big willow tree whose branches drooped down to kiss the water. It was a remarkably beautiful scene, actually. The trees, the little puffs of cloud reflected in the pond, the reeds and grass that bent in the wind along the banks.

And the T-Rex, gazing out across the modern landscape with its glittering prehistoric eye.

She had figured out from there which buildings must be the Ranch, and now she turned from the dusty country road down an even dustier unmarked driveway. It led down a small incline and then up and over a hill. The picturesque pond and willow tree from Google Maps was just about half a mile down the road on the same side; she could see it, faintly, from here.

Tallulah knew from her scrutiny of the map that the Ranch was beyond the hill, and yet her heart beat hard and fast as she thought about cresting that ridge. What if she was wrong? Or worse: what if she was right, and the Ranch had set up a security perimeter of dinosaurs that could crush her Kia flat?

She glanced at her driver's side mirror. OBJECTS IN MIRROR ARE CLOSER THAN THEY APPEAR. "I guess I'll see you if you're comin'," she said out loud with a laugh, and began to drive.

Everything was silent. Even the dusty wind seemed oddly still as she slowly drove down into the dip, then up towards the top of the hill.

At the crest, she had to take a moment to stare.

The hill was not just a hill, but rather the edge of a huge bowl, probably a mile or more across, that was full of strange vegetation. Bushes the size of trees. Plants with enormous fan-shaped leaves, bigger than six of her laid end-to-end. Tall grasses gone to seed, higher than her head, and massive, primitive-looking reeds that ringed a circular pond - more like a lake - in the center. It was incredibly beautiful, and also faintly disturbing in its uncanniness, as if she was looking directly into the distant past of this patch of land, millions of years ago.

And then there was an alarm.

It started as a flash of impossibly bright light, which was followed by a loud, animal shriek. Faintly, she could hear a bell ringing from a building that she hadn't noticed, low and squat and hidden among the leaves and reeds.

Tallulah braced herself. For what, she wasn't quite sure, but it didn't sound good. *Wits about you, Chicken,* she thought. *Let's just ride this out and see.*

Three black cars sped towards her on a track that emerged from the jungled bowl. They stopped a dozen feet from the Kia, and a tall, muscled man emerged from one. His face was a dark cloud, and his body was taut and ready for a fight.

He was the most beautiful man Tallulah had ever seen.

There was another flash of bright light, and then everything was dark.

CHAPTER 3

Tallulah awoke slowly to the sound of voices in another room. She couldn't quite make out what they were saying, but one sounded contrite. The other, booming and deep, was angry. Not explosively so; he was clearly keeping his anger in check. But he was not happy.

Eyes still closed, she wiggled her fingers and toes. Everything seemed to be in working order. She shifted her body and found herself at the edge of a comfortable mattress, head cradled by a soft pillow. She opened her eyes slowly, as the light in the room was bright - sunshine, she saw, as it streamed in from a large window set into the wall across from the bed.

A large, *barred* window.

Tallulah swung her legs over the edge of the bed, pausing briefly to let the spinning sensation pass, and tentatively stood up. Her body seemed undamaged, to her relief. The room was small, with four cot-style beds and two desks, nothing on the walls except a standard schoolroom-style clock, and a heavy-looking door.

She grabbed the doorknob and tried to turn it. Locked.

As she rattled the doorknob, the voices in the other room immediately stopped. "Hello?" she called out.

After all, if they were going to kill her, they'd probably have done so already. She'd learned that from all the action films she'd watched with her dad over the years, him in his favorite recliner and her on the couch, passing a bowl of popcorn between them.

If she was alive and unharmed, she was valuable to them in some way.

You bet your ass I'm valuable, she thought. *I'm gonna be a paleontologist and I'm at the top of my class.*

There was movement from the other room, and then a key in the lock. "Get away from the door," the deep voice said. "I don't want you coming out here without my permission."

"Yes, sir," said Tallulah sweetly.

After a moment, the door swung open. In the doorway stood the man from the car.

He was tall - at least six foot three - and muscled like a fighter. His shoulders were broad and strong in his casual T-shirt, and his powerful legs threatened to rip his field khakis apart. He had a slight belly, in the manner of men whose strength is practical rather than for show, but it only made him more intriguing to her.

This was not a vain man. This was a man who *got shit done*.

His hair was chin-length and straight, with slightly ragged edges, as if he'd tried to cut it himself and failed so hadn't bothered anymore. It was sandy-blond and sun-streaked like a surfer's. His eyes were a deep blue-grey in a suntanned face that was surprisingly open. His beauty was not cruel or hard, but rather inviting, alluring.

As if he were hungry for the world, and wanted nothing more than to feast on it.

Tallulah had never seen anything so beautiful in her life.

Tallulah and the man sat across from each other at a small table in what passed for a living room at the Ranch. He'd asked the contrite-voiced person, who was small and short-haired and generally amiable, to fetch some coffee for the two of them; rather than ask for milk or sugar, Tallulah drank hers black, looking directly into those blue-grey eyes as she took her first sip.

"Now that you've got me here, can I at least have your name?" she said to the man.

"I don't think you're in any position to be asking much of anything," he said.

"Oh?" Tallulah said. "Last I checked, false imprisonment was a crime."

"So's trespassing." The man took a sip of coffee, and then another, deeper one.

"Touché".

"I'll make you a deal," said the man, his voice rumbling. Tallulah breathed deeply.

"What's that?"

"You can go on your way, no harm no foul, as long as you swear never to come back here. And never to talk about the Ranch."

"I don't think I like that deal," said Tallulah.

"Oh?"

"I came here for a reason, you know."

"And what's that?"

"I want a summer job."

There was immediate shocked laughter from the the kitchen, and an amused smile from the man. "Don't make the girl feel bad," the man called into the kitchen, and then turned back to Tallulah. "Sorry. They're a bit out of practice when it comes to interaction with outsiders."

"Who is that?"

"They're my assistant. Don't worry. They don't mean to be rude."

"They – so they/them, right?"

"That's right," said Reid.

"And what about you?"

He laughed, a deep rumble. "He/him. I'm just a man."

You certainly are, Tallulah thought. His

presence was like a gravity well, drawing her in.

"I need to be clear, though, about something else," said the man. "Did you say you wanted a *summer job*?"

"I did."

"Do you know where you are?"

"If my Google Maps skills are any indication," said Tallulah, "this is the Ranch."

"You are correct," said the man. "But do you know what the Ranch is?"

"You raise dinosaurs in a barn-free lifestyle. You've got the biggest variety of dinos in this part of the country. You've got the only T-Rex hatchery outside of New York and California. And," Tallulah said, "I know it's true, because I saw your *T. rex* on Google Maps."

The man stared at her.

"Street view," Tallulah said. "He was hiding in some trees. The *T. rex*."

The man picked up his coffee cup, considered taking a sip, and put it down again. He sighed heavily, tangling his fingers in his hair, forehead in his palm. "You're no slouch."

"Nope." Tallulah fought the urge to bask in the compliment. *Be professional.*

"Tallulah Cole," he said.

"Wait. How do you know *my* name?"

"It's on your driver's license. I had a look."

"Right."

"Tallulah. You know what scarecrows are, right?"

"I'm from Missouri," she said. "Also, I've seen *The Wizard of Oz.*"

"Think of that T-Rex like a scarecrow. It's a real *T. rex*, all right, but it's not there for its own sake."

"What do you mean?"

The afternoon sun streamed in past gauzy curtains and metal bars, illuminating the room: a few mismatched couches, a coffee table bearing a plastic-looking fern, the small wooden dining table across which they faced each other, a sturdy-looking door to the outside. Nondescript and strangely comfortable.

"I mean," the man said, "that the T-Rex was there to scare off things that are even bigger. *Much* bigger. And even more… carnivorous."

There was silence for a moment as Tallulah pretended that she wasn't panicking on the inside. Gorgeous man aside, what in the world had she gotten herself into?

What in the world - in all of world history - was bigger and more carnivorous than *Tyrannosaurus Rex*?

A small smile teased the corners of the man's mouth. His skin was sun-kissed and his beard-stubble framed a strong jaw and full, wide lips. Tallulah tried hard not to stare. "You sure you still want a summer job at the Ranch?"

Tallulah took a deep breath and fixed her face into a jaunty grin. "That depends. Is there hazard pay?"

The man laughed, and suddenly the tension in the room seemed to melt away, though Tallulah's magnetic attraction to the man rushed in to take its place. He was *so* gorgeous. "I think we can arrange that."

"In that case, yes. I do. Is this my interview?"

"Oh, you've passed your interview," the man said in his deep voice. "It's been a while since we've had someone new on the team. But I think you'll fit in well here. Fearless to a fault. It's not a common trait."

"I'm not a common girl." Tallulah shocked herself with her own boldness.

"That much is apparent," said the man. "Maybe you'll even make it through the whole summer here."

"There's just one thing I need before I accept your offer," Tallulah said, slyly.

"What's that?"

"I can't take a job with someone whose name I don't know."

"Ah, yes," said the man. He held out his hand to shake hers. "Reid Canmore, your new boss. Pleased to make your acquaintance, Tallulah Cole."

CHAPTER 4

*R*eid Canmore.

Tallulah's head spun. Reid Canmore. *The* Reid Canmore. The paleontologist-geneticist who'd sequenced the first complete sample of dinosaur DNA. Whose name was on half the papers she'd read so far in grad school. The pioneer of genetic engineering whose research had solidified the relationship between dinosaurs and modern-day birds, whose lab at MIT had successfully grown, in an ostrich egg, the very first dinosaur embryo to produce a live "chick."

The Reid Canmore who, as far as everyone in the field knew, had died in a helicopter crash seven years before.

The Reid Canmore who, it seemed, had the body of a god, the face of a model and a voice that had a direct line to Tallulah's body.

There was a sudden outburst of squawking outside the window. "Sorry," said Reid as he swiftly got up from the table, "the chicks are calling. Gotta make sure all is copacetic. You're the only woman here at the moment, so you'll have that room to yourself." He quickly tightened the laces of his muddy hiking books and grasped the handle of the door to the outside; there was a brief blue light and a beep, and it clicked open for him. "Doors are bio-locked for the moment, I'm sure you understand. Tomorrow, I'll show you around."

"But…" Tallulah had barely gotten out the syllable, but Reid was already outside, and the door closed behind him, locking Tallulah in.

Tallulah watched as he walked away

from the building, followed intently by about a dozen strange-looking creatures about the size of cocker spaniels. They were scrawny and wrinkled like scaled-up baby birds, with fuzzy patches of what looked like downy feathers, but their size - and elongated snouts where birds would have beaks - demonstrated what they actually were.

Dinosaurs. The first juveniles she'd ever seen alive.

And they clearly *loved* Reid. They clambered all over each other as they followed him and as he tossed bits of meat into their waiting maws. They weren't just competing for the food, however; they eagerly accepted affectionate scratches under the chin and between the eyes, leaning in like puppies. For his part, he seemed to love them right back. He was too far away by now for her to hear him, but the affection he showed to these odd-looking creatures… it sparked something in her own heart, a little fire that began to burn, low but persistent.

"C'mon, you guys," Reid's rumbling voice said faintly, in the midst of the squawking. "I just fed you. Hungry little things, aren't you? Don't worry. I'm here. I'll look after you." His crooning was both strangely comforting and unbelievably alluring. She imagined him talking like that to her. *Hungry little thing, aren't you?* he crooned in her mind, lying next to her in bed. *I'll look after you*, as his hands roamed and his mouth moved on her neck, her shoulders...

"Do you need help figuring out your room?" asked a voice behind her.

Tallulah whirled around, startled. The conciliator in the earlier argument was standing behind her, a water glass in their hand. "I thought you might be thirsty for something other than coffee," they said.

"I'm sorry," said Tallulah, "I don't think we've officially met."

"That's true," they said.

Tallulah squinted at them in the sunlight. They were a little taller than her, with short salt-and-pepper hair and warm brown eyes that were nevertheless wary. "I'm Tallulah," she said.

"I know."

"You know what I've noticed?" said Tallulah. "People here seem to enjoy secrecy about their names. Do you know why that might be?"

"I do," they said.

Tallulah sighed. "Will you tell me your name?"

"You can call me Rowan."

"Rowan. Can you tell me what I'm supposed to do now?"

Rowan set the water glass down on the small dining table, collected the two coffee cups, and started towards the door to the kitchen. "First, shall I tell you what you *shouldn't* do?"

"Please do."

"Do not," said Rowan with emphasis, "under any circumstances, pursue Reid."

A bitter dart of disappointment pierced her rosy image of the handsome paleontologist doting on the dinosaur chicks – followed by a rush of defiance. Surely Reid was an adult with his own mind? She hid both impulses as best she could with a bright grin. "I don't think you'll have to worry about that," she lied.

"That's good," said Rowan, with visible relief.

"He's my boss, after all," said Tallulah. "My interest is strictly professional."

Tallulah spent the next few hours settling in, while Rowan made their excuses and headed out across a field, apparently to take care of some chores. She found that someone - Rowan? Reid? - had brought all of her things from the Kia into "her" room before she'd originally woken up, and she arranged everything neatly: clothes into drawers, laptop and phone chargers plugged in, her favorite framed photo of her with her parents on the bedside table. Sound seemed strangely muted in this room; a few times, she saw shadowed, hulking creatures through the window, but their cries and roars were nearly soundless.

The vibration of their steps, however, was profound. It was like living through a series of tiny earthquakes that seemed to shake, albeit slightly, the very foundations of the world.

Well. Hadn't the return of dinosaurs to the land of the living, after hundreds of millions of years, done exactly that?

And hadn't the sight of Reid Canmore, with his wild hair and his brilliantly blue-green eyes and his broad shoulders that seemed as though they could take the weight of the universe, done the same for *her* world?

"Stop it," she said out loud, startling

herself with the volume of her voice in such a small space. "You have one job. Don't screw it up."

Rowan wasn't her boss. Reid was. He'd said as much. And he was the one she would follow.

She was an ambitious paleontologist in training. But in this moment, all she wanted out of life was a little stroke on the head, like the little chicks. All she wanted was for Reid to croon to her and tell her she was about to be fed. She was suddenly, burningly jealous of the creatures.

And then, as the late-afternoon light turned golden and Tallulah's stomach started to rumble, there was a rattle at the door to the outside from the main room. Reid came in, stomping the dust and dried mud off his boots. "I brought you something," he said, putting a paper bag onto the dining table.

Hungry little thing, aren't you?

Tallulah looked inside. "Peanut butter and jelly sandwiches?"

"I didn't say it was a gourmet something. We eat pretty simply out here," Reid said with a guileless smile.

"How do you know I'm not allergic to peanuts?"

"If you are," he said companionably, "I'll get you something else."

His sheer presence was almost intolerably seductive. His forearms were taut with corded muscle, his hands large and powerful. There was a watchfulness, a sharp intelligence, in his eyes that belied his calm demeanor. Tallulah's body cried out to her. She wanted nothing more in the world than to sit and eat sandwiches with this man and to gaze at him while she ate, and then to invite him into the bedroom afterwards.

She had also been warned, very specifically, against doing so, by Rowan.

And by the fact that Reid was supposed

to be dead.

And she was a professional, wasn't she? She was going to be a paleontologist. Field life would always bring her a quotient of attractive, unavailable men.

She decided that she would start as she meant to go on: a perfect lady. She swallowed hard and did her best to push down the wild desire that had grown in her.

"This is perfectly fine, thanks," she said. She grabbed a sandwich and took a huge, unladylike bite. "Dibs on this one."

As they ate, Reid told Tallulah about the land on which the Ranch had been built. "You know the concept of terraforming?" he said. "Taking an inhospitable landscape on another planet and making it suitable for human life? We did something like that here, except we took the landscape and made it suitable for dinosaur life."

"How?" Tallulah asked. "How did you know what they needed? And how did you create it?"

"There was a lot of trial and error," said Reid. "A lot of failures."

"You mean… you experimented on the dinosaurs?"

"No!" Reid cried, genuinely appalled. "Of course not. I love these dinos like I love… well, I don't have children, and perhaps it's not quite the same, but I love them like I loved my dogs as a child. They're my family. My only family," he said quickly, and then seemed to regret it; Tallulah didn't push him. "No, I experimented with the landscape. Creating localized humidity. Adding nutrients to the soil. I collaborated with a team of paleo-botanists in Arizona and Brazil to find the closest modern descendants of prehistoric plants that would be appropriate for the herbivorous dinosaurs to eat, and that would make all of the dinosaurs feel comfortable."

"How do you know if they're comfortable?" asked Tallulah.

"Dinosaurs are large, complex animals," Reid said with a smile. "You just need a bit of empathy. I can tell already that you've got plenty; you care how others feel."

I know how I'd like to make you *feel,* Tallulah didn't say. A hard rush of need came over her; she camouflaged it with a cough.

This would be difficult to do all summer.

"Once you get to know them, you'll be able to tell how they're feeling," Reid continued. "I've gotten pretty good at it."

His smile illuminated his eyes. Tallulah was entranced, and also terrified. She had never felt this *pull*. Complex animals, indeed.

"I have a question," she said abruptly, desperate to break the moment lest she launch herself at him with abandon. "Why are you alive?"

"I'm sorry?" Reid said, his sandwich halfway to his mouth.

"The helicopter crash," said Tallulah. "Everyone said you died. CNN said you died. I remember, because I'd just gotten into Washington University for earth sciences. I hadn't read any of your papers yet, but I remember the crash."

"Mmm," said Reid.

"I remember the wreckage," Tallulah continued. "The helicopter was on fire. They said there were no survivors."

"Mmm," said Reid.

Tallulah stopped. Reid looked at her, silently, a faint grin on his face.

"Do I look dead?" he asked.

"I mean, no," said Tallulah. "But dinosaurs *did* look dead for a minimum of sixty-five million years, and now you've got a gaggle of them who follow you around your hidden *Fern Gully* forest in rural Missouri, so maybe my perception is a little bit off."

"Tallulah." Reid popped the last bit of his sandwich into his mouth, chewed slowly, and washed it down with a swig of water. Golden sunlight beamed directly into his eyes; he squinted and shielded them with his hand, peering at her from the shadow. His beauty was nearly unbearable. "Do you trust me?"

"No," she said, pulling herself together, being deliberately sharp. "I don't. I'm intrigued by you. I think you're a genius. I think you're magnetic –" *mayday!* she thought, panicking – "magnetic to, uh, your little dino buddies. They seem to love you. They're really into you."

"They are, indeed, really into me," chuckled Reid, amused. "You're familiar with the avian process of imprinting, yes?"

"Of course," she said. "Wait. So you're their... dad?"

"Sort of," said Reid. "It's more complicated than that. But they trust me completely." He looked at her expectantly.

"I'm sorry," said Tallulah. "I'm just being honest. I'm sure I'll trust you at some point."

"There's no need to apologize." Reid got up from the table and took their water glasses to refill in the kitchen. "If you trusted me already," he called over the running faucet, "I'd think you were naïve."

"Like a baby dinosaur," Tallulah called back.

Reid turned off the tap and brought two full glasses of water back to the table. "You'll have to forgive me if I'm a little unused to human company," he confessed as he sat back down. "Other than the operational staff, It's mostly just me and the dinos out here."

"And Rowan, right?"

"Ah, yes. Rowan." Reid sighed and

leaned back in his chair. "Rowan is the glue that holds this place together. They're so useful that I overlook how irritating they can be."

"They seem perfectly nice to me," said Tallulah.

"Just smile and nod," said Reid. "You'll get along fine."

Tallulah smiled and nodded, to illustrate the concept. "The helicopter," she reminded him. "You were going to tell me why the entire world thought you died in a helicopter crash, but you're alive and having dinner with me. Speaking of trust."

There was a long silence as Reid drank his entire glass of water in small, deliberate gulps. He slammed the glass down on the table jovially, as though it had been a beer. "Alright, Tallulah Cole," he said. "I promised you a tour tomorrow. Get some rest, and be ready to go by eight AM. Your questions will be answered."

Before she could protest, he was already out the door, giving her a friendly smile and a small wave as he bio-locked her in for the night.

CHAPTER 5

Even in the darkest days of junior high school, Tallulah had never before had such an existential crisis as to what to wear.

It was seven fifty-five AM, she'd been up for two hours, and still, everything she'd brought with her felt wrong. Her wide-leg khakis felt too frumpy, her black leggings too urban. Shorts? She thought despairingly of her razor, currently sitting on the lip of the sink in her Airbnb in Independence, forgotten in a frenzy of packing. And the shirts! One by one, she tossed them aside: too loose, too boxy, too long. What had she been thinking, bringing a silk blouse? She crumpled it up and tossed it into the corner in annoyance; a moment later, contrite, she hung it on one of three wire hangers in a small closet that clearly hadn't been aired out in a while.

Finally, she settled on a thick olive-green jersey romper she'd worn for fieldwork in Arizona the previous summer. It was shorts, yes, but her legs weren't *that* stubbly yet. And she was proud of her legs, to be honest; she hadn't skipped leg day in months. She'd just hope that Reid wouldn't notice any stubble. Maybe he'd just be glad to see a woman's legs at all, since she was the only woman there.

Maybe he wasn't interested in women at all. Maybe he had some kind of complicated relationship with Rowan, and that's why they'd warned her off. Maybe he was interested in *dinosaurs*.

The thought sent her into a fit of nervous giggles. Maybe that was what he'd meant by dinosaur imprinting being "complicated". This was a world where dinosaurs had been brought back from the dead, millions of years later, and one of the world's leading paleontologists had been brought back from the dead seven years later. How could she eliminate any possibilities, really?

She was finishing up her five-minute fieldwork makeup routine – SPF tinted moisturizer and lip balm, gel eyeliner, a bit of mascara – when there was a knock at the door to her room. "Are you decent?" asked Reid's deep voice.

"I'm not sure about that," said Tallulah with a laugh, "but I'm dressed and ready to go." *A little flirting won't harm anyone, will it?*

Reid opened the door, and Tallulah nearly had to avert her eyes at the sight of him. Just his presence was enough to make her nipples harden and her breath quicken.

He was wearing the same jeans as the day before, but with a breezy cream linen button-down shirt that skimmed every muscle in his shoulders and arms. His hair was silky and his face was freshly shaven. As she walked past him towards the door to the outside, she caught his scent: clean, somehow both bright and deep, like a glacier-fed spring in the middle of a forest. And there was something else underneath it: something primordial and essential, like life itself.

The possibility occurred to her that he had also made an effort for *her*.

She felt dizzy.

"Helicopter's waiting," he said, and gestured her through the door.

The helicopter was, indeed, waiting, its blades spinning. The same helicopter she'd seen on CNN reduced to crumpled tin in the middle of a field, flames licking the rotors, seven years before. She recognized the red stripe down the side, thinning gradually to a point where it met the tail.

"How?" Tallulah shouted. Reid handed her a set of ear protectors and set his finger to his lips in the universal "shhh" motion. The gesture pulled at something deep within her; she quashed a wild impulse to pull him back towards the bedroom, and stomped onwards determinedly in her field boots, the helicopter's wind whipping her bare legs.

They ducked their heads and climbed in; Reid helped boost her into the seat next to his, and she followed his lead as she buckled herself in. The pilot, a grey-haired man with a jovial smile, gave them the thumbs-up before turning back to the controls.

Reid reached up to his right ear, and pulled down a small mic that had been tucked into his ear protector. Before Tallulah could do the same, he reached across and did it for her. His hand, rough and warm, brushed her cheek; she allowed her eyes to flutter closed for a split second and imagined that, perhaps, he had lingered there just a little longer than was strictly necessary. Warmth pulsed between her legs, frustratingly. "Testing," said his voice in her ears. "Testing. One, two."

"Roger that," she said. "I think that's correct."

He shook his head. "Testing, one, two," he said again.

She pointed at her mic and shook her head. "I don't think it's working."

Reid looked quizzical for a moment, and then unbuckled his upper body from the restraint. He leaned far over until his face was almost touching hers. His mouth was inches from her mic, and from her lips. "Testing, one, two," he whispered softly.

There was nothing in the world Tallulah wanted more than to pull him towards her and kiss him.

And then there was a high, piercing squeal of feedback in both of their ears.

Reid jerked back into his seat. "I'm so sorry," he whispered into the mic. "Try again?"

"That was… unpleasant," said Tallulah, a little dazed.

"I can hear you now," said Reid. "I'm sorry for getting so close. I won't do it again. It was purely to try to fix the issue."

"Oh, gosh, I didn't mean… I meant the sound was unpleasant," stammered Tallulah. "It's OK. It wasn't unpleasant to have you close… it's okay, you did what you needed to do. You did what you wanted to do. What you had to do? Oh my God, you fixed the problem and that was great and I appreciate it and it wasn't at all unpleasant. Except the sound. It's fine. I'm fine. I'm good. You're good. You're really good." She looked down, and then out the window, trying to compose herself.

You're a professional. A paleontologist. Almost. Paleontologists don't freak out about helicopters or unavailable men or both.

"Well, now that that's settled, would you like to know why we're in this helicopter?" asked Reid, gentle amusement in his voice.

"I most certainly would."

"So here's the thing," Reid said. He paused a moment to look out the window, and then brought his gaze back to her. His green eyes were piercing. "Ironically, it's sometimes a whole lot safer to be dead than alive."

As they flew a survey over Dino Ranch, Reid launched into the story, from the beginning.

"I was born into a minor branch of an old family. My great-grandfather was the Baron of Illingsford, a small English estate near the Welsh border. Like a lot of nobles, his name was worth more than his bank account, so he married the daughter of a wealthy American manufacturing magnate. They called them Dollar Princesses: the Americans provided the money, the English provided the title. Their son, my grandfather, came to Harvard to study mathematics, but he had a lot of difficulty fitting in with the American side of the family, and there were a lot of awkward and difficult dinners at their home on Beacon Hill…"

"You know," Tallulah interrupted, "you don't seem much like a Baron of Illingsford. I don't know a lot of English nobles who would spend their time in rural Missouri as a… dinosaur cowboy. On a ranch."

Reid seemed taken aback. "I promise you, it's true."

"Oh, I don't doubt that. But I personally think 'world-famous applied paleontologist and dinosaur geneticist' is much more impressive than 'descendant of minor English baron'".

Reid rubbed his forehead, seeming a bit bewildered. "People are usually keen on the nobility thing."

"Yeah, I'm not impressed by who your ancestors are. I'm impressed by who *you* are. I didn't sleuth this place out for a summer job with the Baron of Bumblefucking-hamshire. I wanted a job with whoever was obsessed enough with dinosaurs to build this place."

"Well," said Reid, "that's where the money came from to build this place. My family. And they've all passed on now, so I suppose it's mine."

"And what about the dinosaurs?" asked Tallulah. "How did you get interested in them?"

"My mother was a geneticist," he said. "She made the connection between DNA and topology, my dad's field of math. She thought maybe my dad could help her develop mathematical models for DNA to repair it. She was way ahead of her time."

"And she did."

"Yep. At some point, a couple of pale-ontologists found a bone fragment in a peat bog with enough DNA to be workable for my mother's process. My father helped her build the model, but she was really the lead. If it wasn't for her, we wouldn't have dinosaurs hanging around this forest."

"So why does everyone think Jameson and Okoye brought the dinosaurs back? When it was really her?"

Reid snorted. "Why does everyone think Watson and Crick discovered DNA?" he asked rhetorically. "It's not about who did it, it's about who took credit for it. At least Ikemba Okoye tried to get my mother's name on the paper. But Jameson refused. And he threatened to cut out Okoye, too, and to have him deported. It was terrible."

"Makes me want to update a couple of Wikipedia pages," Tallulah said with a hint of a smile.

A cloud of emotion – was it fear? – darkened Reid's beautiful face for a brief moment, then it passed. "Please don't," he said. "I'd like to let things lie."

"Is this why you're safer dead than alive?"

"Oh, no," said Reid. "That's a different... family situation." His tone made it clear that this was a conversation for later on.

The helicopter began to descend slowly onto a square patch of close-cut field grass between the lake and a large copse of huge-leafed trees. There was a bump as it touched down. Tallulah jolted forward in her seat, and Reid reached out an arm to steady her, his hand on her shoulder. She went very still, hoping he'd keep it there – and he did, as the rotors slowed and the din of the helicopter quieted. He gestured out the window towards the trees.

"And here we are, Tallulah Cole. Are you ready to see your first live dinosaurs?" He gestured towards the forest.

"We have a couple in our lab at Mizzou," said Tallulah almost regretfully. "And I saw you with the juveniles last night."

Reid chuckled. "Ah, yes, my summer assistant is a *doctoral student*. Right, then. Tallulah, are you ready to see your first *free-range* live dinosaurs?"

"Ready when you are, boss." Tallulah saluted, cocking her hip in what she hoped was a subtly flirtatious way.

Those blue-grey eyes crinkled, those muscles moved beneath the white shirt and jeans. Tallulah could barely breathe, so beautiful was the sight. Reid pointed towards a path that cut efficiently into the vegetation. "Right this way, then."

CHAPTER 6

"I don't see anything," said Tallulah, squinting into the fern-filled underbrush.

They'd been walking for at least fifteen minutes, maybe twenty, batting aside branches and giant leaves. The path through the woods was narrow and lined with packed-down prairie soil. Despite the density of the trees, Tallulah saw how the dappled light illuminated bark and branches and the curled ferns that grew as high as her waist. She watched as specks of dust danced languorously in the sunbeams.

She saw how Reid's eyes scanned the forest, how the muscles in his back moved gorgeously under the linen of his shirt. She saw how he walked gracefully, almost like a cat, lithe despite his powerful size. It was difficult not to imagine him leading her into the forest, laying her down on a bed of leaves, pinning her down with those power-ful forearms...

What she didn't see was dinosaurs.

"Patience, Tallulah," Reid said. His voice was warm with humour. "They're around."

When Tallulah was a young teen, her parents had taken her to Seattle on a whale-watching trip. There had been two days of staring balefully at the watery hori-zon before they'd encountered any whales – but when they'd finally appeared, a huge family of humpbacks cresting and jumping and swimming like hulking shadows beside the boat, she finally understood why people willingly spend so much time and money and effort to see them.

"Maybe it's like the whales," murmured

Tallulah.

"Hm?" Reid stopped. "Whales?"

"Oh, just a memory. My family went –"

"Shhhhh," whispered Reid, cutting her off and putting his hand on her shoulder, gently, for emphasis. "Look there." He pointed to their left with his other hand, perpendicular to the path. "Don't move. Don't talk. Just look."

But you're touching me, thought Tallulah. *How can I think of anything else?* She moved subtly closer to him, shifting her weight against his hand, and looked into the shaded brush.

At first she wondered if he'd been seeing things. Everything was so very still and quiet. A cicada trilled brightly in a tree nearby, and was joined by another; the rest was silence.

And then, when she had almost given up, she caught a glimpse of movement – not leaves or branches, but rather a sudden swirl in the motes of dust that floated in a wide sunbeam about three dozen feet from the path, not too far off the ground.

Then there was a sudden shake, and a bony head poked through the narrow gap between two of the giant leaf-fronds. It nibbled at one of them idly, then sauntered through, shredding the leaf's edges with the dull spiky protrusions that grew from a complex of armored plates along its back and sides.

"Here, boy," Reid said softly, his voice full of joy. "You've gotten big. Look at you. Look at you."

"Ankylosaurus," whispered Tallulah reverently.

The armored creature swiveled its head to look at them. "How you doing, boy?" said Reid. "There you go. You're a good boy."

It was clearly a juvenile. Its tallest point, the crest of its back, was barely higher than Tallulah's waist, and its spikes were clearly still in the process of growing. Despite the weight of its bony armor, it was surprisingly light on its feet, stepping carefully through the forest. Sunlight dappled its bone-covered face.

The small dinosaur started towards Tallulah and Reid, stopping after a few steps to nibble on a fern leaf. Tallulah's awe was suddenly shot through with fear. Even a juvenile Ankylosaur, she knew, could crush a human's skull with its clubbed tail or its bony forehead.

"Are you sure this is safe?" Tallulah asked Reid in a low voice.

"Safe?" he repeated. "Of course not. But if you wanted a safe summer job, I'm guessing you wouldn't have spent all that energy to find us here." She looked away from the dinosaur and up at his face; he was still gazing into the forest, but he was smiling, his eyes crinkled with good humor. He was dazzling. "And this guy certainly isn't going to eat you. Just keep your feet out from under his. He's still a bit like a puppy: young and clumsy."

"I always wanted a puppy when I was a kid," said Tallulah. "My parents are both allergic, even though I'm not. So I had a fish."

"Tallulah wants a puppy," laughed Reid. "Noted."

Before she could respond, the Ankylosaur lifted its head and trotted towards Reid. "There you go, buddy," Reid cooed. Tallulah stood totally still, frozen with fear and anticipation, her heart still hammering. But the dinosaur had no interest in her. It only had eyes for Reid. She watched as it approached him, leaving a little trail of crushed green vegetation in its path. Despite his caution about its clumsiness, it was almost graceful in its movements. Its eyes, on either side of its head, were black and depthless.

When it was close enough, Reid reached out behind the thick, samurai-esque helmet of bone-armor that covered its face and head. He *scratched* it like one would scratch a puppy. The Ankylosaur gave a high-pitched, birdlike coo of what seemed to be happiness or contentment.

"It sounds like a pigeon," said Tallulah softly, "if a pigeon was a dinosaur the size of a wolf."

"That's a pretty good description," said Reid. "Do you want to give it a try?"

"Yes," said Tallulah before she could think twice.

"Here," said Reid. He crouched down and gestured for her to the same, which she did. He took her hand in his, and guided it to a spot on the Ankylosaur's neck where the flared collar of bone met the smooth, scaled skin of its neck. Tallulah was shocked at how warm it was, and how soft. "Even the bone is warm," she murmured.

"That's right," he said. "It's bone, not horn. It has a blood supply. They're sensitive souls. Especially the young ones like this little guy. Right, buddy?"

The Ankylosaur gave another small coo and raised its head, cocking it so that Reid and Tallulah could scratch the side of its neck.

"Did it just talk back to you?" Tallulah asked, astonished.

"Not as such," said Reid. He was still looking at the dinosaur, clearly entranced. She didn't blame him; the thing was *cute* in a way that she'd never expected a dino to be. "They don't have language, per se, like we do. But they're thinking, feeling beings, and they have some level of intelligence. I want them to have a happy life here."

They were silent, amid the chorus of forest cicadas that had started up again. The Ankylosaur was snuffling gently, its breath making the leaves rustle at the edge of the path.

Tallulah settled back on her heels and

reached her hand underneath the dino's chin, leaning against Reid so that the left side of her back was pressed against the right side of his chest. The feel of his taut body against hers was a revelation. The bony warmth of the dinosaur was fascinating, but even that fascination receded into the background as her entire awareness focused on the sensation of being this close to Reid.

She breathed in deeply. His scent was sawdust and woodsmoke and mountain spring and that same *something else* she couldn't identify. His body seemed connected to hers by that electric attraction that roared up from the deepest parts of her animal self, honed by billions of years of evolution into this. The desire to live, to bring new life into the world – and in doing so, to touch, to taste, to take. She wanted to kiss every part of his body. She wanted to know every bit of him. To feel his body against her, to hear him murmur to her in that impossibly deep voice. She wanted him to crush her, to lift her, to have her.

Professional, dammit. Professional!

The dinosaur craned its head towards her so that it was looking her in the eye. "Crrr?" it cooed, like a question. Its dark eye glimmered with – what? Intelligence? Interest? Some unfathomable dinosaur humor? Tallulah saw now that what she'd taken for ink-blackness was actually a pupil, adjusted to the relative dark of the forest, ringed by a deep gray-green iris flecked with gold.

"Beautiful, isn't it? The eye?" Reid murmured.

"Unbelievably." Her voice was barely above a whisper.

"I think he likes you."

"I like him," said Tallulah. "I really, really like him."

Reid hadn't made any moves to get closer to her, Tallulah noticed with exquisite frustration. But he hadn't shifted away from her, either. Her body had become a heat map: blue and cool where it met the forest air, hot electric red where she touched him. She tried to keep her breathing steady. If she gave in to her desire now, it would be difficult to climb back out.

Besides: she was going to be a *paleontologist*. She was seeing a dinosaur in the wild for the first time. With her boss. She owed it to herself and her career to bring some professionalism to this moment.

With enormous difficulty and much internal protest, she moved away from Reid and stood up, brushing dust from the backs of her legs. "This is incredibly cool," she said brightly. She offered her hand to Reid, to help him up. "Can you show me more?"

The forest, it turned out, was full of dinosaurs.

Little herds of turkey-sized *Albertadromeus*, cheeping and squawking as they ran through the undergrowth. A single enormous *Iguanodon* like a hulking shadow in the distant trees. A few duck-billed

Protohadros in a cluster by a wide creek that bisected the path about a half hour into their walk. "I keep meaning to get a bridge built here," Reid said as they picked their way across the burbling water on flat-topped stones.

Only herbivores, of course. The carnivores and omnivores, Reid explained, had their own enclosed territories. ("They're still free-range," he said, "but there are safety limits to that.") Tallulah remembered seeing what had looked like high-walled pastures from the helicopter; she'd figured they were some kind of dinosaur enclosure, and it was nice to know she was right. Perhaps she was a professional after all.

If only Reid wasn't so *magnetic*.

It was an unfamiliar feeling for Tallulah. At twenty-five, she'd had boyfriends, but none of them had held her interest for more than a year or so. Her high school sweetheart had been a lovely, simple boy called Tobin, tall and sandy-haired and shy. He was a perfect gentleman who knew all the right things to say and do, and in the end it left her cold: there was no spontaneity, no passion. He'd married a girl from church a few years ago, and she'd sent a gift when their baby was born two years ago, relieved that it hadn't been her.

Freshman year of college there'd been Hunter, a lacrosse player who'd pressured her to diet and stop lifting weights because he preferred "his girls" to be slender rather than broad and muscular; once she'd extricated herself from the brief relationship, she'd vowed never to betray herself like that again.

And she hadn't.

From then on, it had been an occasional series of months-long entanglements. She was pretty, she knew, but she was short and powerfully muscled and wasn't very good at playing dumb or fawning over men, and that was what a lot of the Mizzou boys seemed to want. Omondi, a Kenyan exchange student obsessed with paleo-botany who'd been in her advanced statistics seminar her senior year, had been her favorite of all of them; he'd listened carefully when she spoke excitedly about her research assistantship with the department chair, and taught her about the native plants in Kenya. But he'd gone back home just after Christmas, she'd already been offered admission into the PhD program, and they both knew their tearful airport goodbye was likely to be their last.

Since Omondi had left, it had just been Tallulah and her dinosaur bones. Tallulah and her dinosaur DNA. Tallulah and her dinosaur research.

And now, Tallulah and her dinosaur-loving boss. Who happened to be the most attractive human being she'd ever seen with her own eyes, whose simple presence made her weak.

It was a problem, she knew. She should try to keep it tamped down. But still an old excitement had welled up in her, a hopefulness she hadn't felt in a very long time – and quickly, it had become a wild, nearly uncontrollable desire. It was the longing for something both real and lasting, for a connection that was mutual, with someone who shared her interests and passions and dreams for the future, and whose body was its own fascinating country that she was desperate to explore…

"You doing alright, Tallulah Cole?" asked Reid gently. She startled as he put his hand gently on her arm. "Just daydreaming?"

"Oh, I'm fine," she said quickly. "Sorry. Just thinking about the dinosaurs." She matched her stride to his. His hand lingered on her arm just a little longer than necessary.

"There'll be plenty of time for that," he chuckled. "We're almost back at the helicopter. We can recap there."

"Recap," Tallulah repeated.

"Yes. We'll review the sightings today, and discuss what the rest of the week looks like, dinosaur-wise. And downtime-wise." His smile lit up his face.

"I was going to ask about that." Tallulah tried to seem casual. "What do y'all do in the evenings here? I can't imagine there's much nightlife in Norborne."

"You're right about that," said Reid. "Though we don't leave the ranch at all, so it's moot. But we make our own fun. You'll see. I'll make sure you're looked after."

Was he… flirting?

There was nothing in the world – nothing in the universe – Tallulah wanted more than to make her own fun with Reid Canmore, legendary paleontologist and official dead man. But what she said was: "I look forward to it." There. Calm. Strictly professional.

For as long as she could manage, anyway.

CHAPTER 7

The first thing Tallulah noticed when she got back to her room was that her phone was gone.

She felt sick and hot and scared. Had she accidentally taken it into the helicopter and dropped it? Into the forest? An image came unbidden to her mind: her shiny phone, her lifeline to the outside world, crushed into shards of glass and bits of twisted metal under the heavy foot of the *Iguanodon*. But no – she pushed it away. She *knew* she'd left her phone here on its charger, next to the bed, where it always was. The charger still lay there, plugged into the wall with a little coiled tail of covered wire and no phone at the end of it.

Another unbidden thought: *how can I call for help?*

And another, more forbidden: *maybe if I "disappear," Reid and I can pretend to be dead together, among the dinosaurs, and get in touch with our animal instincts…*

Now that she was alone, Tallulah finally gave in to the rush of desire. She lay down on the bed and let her own hands roam, let herself feel it everywhere in her body. She imagined Reid laying her down in the forest on a soft bed of leaves, or in the helicopter, or in this bed, touching her and kissing her and stroking her hair, reaching down between her legs and putting his strong hands to work…

"Don't worry," said Rowan's voice outside her door, jolting Tallulah from her thoughts. She sat up quickly, blushing furiously. "Your phone is safe. We just don't allow them here. Can't risk information getting out."

"Um," said Tallulah, flustered and blushing. "Uh. Thank you. Sorry. Okay. Sorry, just give me a minute?"

She went into the bathroom, ran the tap and splashed herself with a faceful of freezing water. The shock of the cold was enough to break the spell of her imagination long enough for her to get it under control. She looked in the mirror, which now bore a fine spray of water droplets. The water hadn't done much to calm the redness in her cheeks, it seemed, but it had washed most of the dust and sweat away. Her eyes were bright, their meadow-green contrasting with the flush on her cheekbones, and her lips were quirked in a little smile. Water streamed down a few stray locks of hair that escaped from her ponytail during their adventure; it beaded at the ends and dripped dark splotches onto the breast of her jumpsuit.

Tallulah rolled her shoulders back and stood straight. She would never be tall, she knew. She'd always have these broad shoulders and heavy muscles. But those muscles would carry her through a summer of hiking through forests and flying in helicopters and chasing after dinosaurs.

They were good for other physical activities, too; Reid certainly hadn't minded the feel of her shoulder, or her arm, or her back against him...

Enough for now.

"Okay," she called. "I'm coming out."

She emerged from the room to find Rowan standing in the living room along with two men she didn't recognize. The three were clustered near the dining table, chatting in low voices and sipping from large white mugs. Rowan looked up when they heard Tallulah open the door.

"Enjoy your flight?" they asked with a half-smile.

"It certainly was interesting," smiled Tallulah. "Do I get to meet more of the team now?"

"Sure do. That's Nico," they said, pointing at the taller man, "and that's James." The short, blandly handsome man gave her a friendly smile. Both were wearing jeans and dark grey polo tees, each with a small embroidered animal on the left breast.

Tallulah squinted. "Are those… Lacoste polos? But with dinosaurs?"

Nico grinned. One of his canine teeth was missing. "Sorority girl?"

"Absolutely not." Tallulah tried to sound offended. The truth was that she'd rushed and joined Alpha Omega Epsilon, but quit during sophomore year when the grueling schedule of parties became too much. She was, as much as she hated to admit it to herself, too much of an introvert. "Dinosaurs are my sorority."

"I didn't know they had a dino sorority," said Nico. "Cool."

"This is the uniform," James said.

Lola Faust

"You'll get one tomorrow, probably. They're nice, eh?"

"Very subtle. I like it," said Tallulah. "Rowan, where's yours?"

Rowan looked down at their black T-shirt and jeans, the same outfit they'd been wearing earlier. They shrugged. "I guess I forgot."

"Where's Reid?" asked Tallulah.

The two men exchanged an unreadable split-second glance, but Tallulah caught it. "He's in the enclosure with the big guys," Nico said.

"Next question. When do I get my phone back?"

Rowan shifted uncomfortably. "At the end of the summer, or the end of your work term with us. Whichever comes first."

"And you do this instead of a simple non-disclosure agreement because…?"

"Because," said Rowan, "the remedies

100

for breaking an NDA are usually financial. There's no amount of money in the world that could fix the issues that would arise if we were found out."

"You do realize there's a Buzzfeed article about you, right…?"

Rowan's eyes went wide. "There's a *what?*"

"A Buzzfeed article. Here, let me show –" Tallulah was halfway towards reaching for her phone in her back pocket, instinctively, before stopping short. "Right. I can't show you. Just Google this place and scroll down to about the sixth or seventh page."

Rowan set their mouth in a hard line and exhaled through their nose, hard. "James," they said. "Can you go off-prop and call the rep management guys? It's still Donovan. You know the protocol."

"Yep." James set his mug on the table and bent down to pull his boots on. "Should I use the main phone?"

"Use #4 for this, please. Use the Laroche path to get yourself back on-prop once you're done."

"Roger that." James gave Rowan a little salute and then flashed a white-toothed grin at Tallulah. "Sorry to leave you so quick. I'm sure we'll have lots of time to chat this summer."

"All good," said Tallulah, mystified. Once James had walked out the door, she looked at Rowan. "Is he getting the article taken down from Google or something?"

"You could say something like that," Rowan said. "We take our privacy here at the Ranch very, very seriously."

"Does it have something to do with the fact that Reid is supposed to be dead?"

Rowan's eyes flashed. Nico leaned against the table and took a long sip from his mug. "There are layers here," said Rowan. "It sounds like Reid's filled you in on some of the basics."

"I have no doubt it's complicated," Tallulah said.

"I want you to listen very, very carefully to me right now," said Rowan, looking directly into Tallulah's eyes. Their gaze was steely and unforgiving. If this was Rowan's demeanor when they were giving instructions, Tallulah decided, then she didn't want to be on the other end of it when they were actually angry.

"I'm listening," she said, putting as much sincerity into her voice as she could.

"All of this, every wall and barrier and limitation and boundary we've put into place, is to protect Reid. It exists to make sure he's safe and that he can do his life's work. Everything else is secondary. What matters here, what is of *paramount importance*, is the health and safety of Reid Canmore."

"I understand." She wanted him safe and well as much as any of them, if for different reasons.

"Do you?" Rowan cocked their head. "Do you, really?"

"I mean, I think so?" Tallulah shifted her weight uncomfortably from one foot to the other. "Is there anything specific you need me to do? Reid seems like he's pretty competent at looking after himself."

"Here's what you can do," said Rowan. "Follow the rules. Listen to what I tell you to do. Listen to the other staff members. Forget about your phone while you're here. Just do your job."

"I can do that."

"And sign this contract and waiver." Rowan reached into a leather tote bag sitting on one of the dining chairs, pulled out a manila envelope, and gave it to Tallulah.

She opened the envelope and pulled out three sheets of paper. "I expected something longer, maybe?" she said, surprised.

Rowan laughed. "You're a summer student," they said. "This covers pretty much everything you'll be doing."

Tallulah pulled out one of the chairs at the dining table and sat down to read. Nico moved aside and picked up his mug. "I'll leave this in the sink," he said to Rowan. "Shall I see if James needs any help?"

"He'll be fine," said Rowan. "But Robbie was going to re-wire the panels in the dry lab. Why don't you help with the calculations?"

Nico nodded and slipped out the door as Tallulah scanned the contract. She was no lawyer, but her mother's best friend was a litigator, and she'd absorbed enough from Auntie Sar's courtroom stories at their weekly Sunday dinners to know her liabilities from her liens. The contract was written fairly plainly, in any case. Act in the best interests of the employer: check. Adhere to all policies, procedures, rules and regulations: check. *Employee shall perform all duties to the best of their ability, including duties not specified.*

She could think of some duties she'd like to perform.

Focus, Tallulah.

But she wasn't a lawyer. Maybe she'd call her mom and see if Auntie Sar was there. She often was, now that she'd retired.

"Just one question," Tallulah said. "Can I please call my parents? Or at least let them know that I'm safe?"

"Don't worry," Rowan held out their hand for the paperwork. "They know you're okay."

"How…?"

"Listen," Rowan said firmly. "Do you want this job or not?"

"Yes," said Tallulah. "I do." *And this boss.*

"Then trust the process and let it go."

Tallulah was a scientist. She was, by and large, a rational person. She knew that signing a contract without legal advice was a bad idea, and that dinosaurs could be as dangerous as they were fascinating. She knew, deep in her bones, that this was a risky endeavor.

For a few long moments, she considered tearing up the contract and asking to leave. She imagined driving her little blue Kia up the driveway and away from the Ranch forever.

But that would take her away from Reid. She couldn't stand the thought. She'd barely known him for a day, but she was hooked.

And how did she know they would even let her leave?

What had happened between when she'd fainted on arrival and when she'd woken up in the bedroom?

"What happens if I don't sign? If I want to leave?"

Rowan smiled tightly. "You'll be unharmed, don't worry. But is that the choice you want to make? Or do you want to trust the process and let it go?"

Her heart pounded in her ears; her throat was swollen with fear.

Not just fear – *anticipation*.

If she signed this contract, she'd be trapped on this dinosaur ranch for the summer. The only woman on staff. Studying dinosaur genetics and husbandry. Under the supervision of Reid Canmore, brilliant paleontologist and most beautiful man she'd ever seen.

"Hand me a pen?" she said. "I'm in."

"Don't touch that, Tallulah!" Reid called out to her from across the lab. "There's a sign. DON'T TOUCH. I thought it was clear, but please tell me if you're having difficulty with it and we can figure out another solution."

"I'm sorry!" cried Tallulah.

Reid made his way around a phalanx of workbenches that held unopened bottles of reagents, ending up by her side. "It's okay," he said good-naturedly. "The nitrile gloves keep it safe from the oils on your hands. And this thing is pretty indestructible. I just don't want to leave anything to chance or to malfunction."

"Are you telling me I have oily hands?" Tallulah teased.

"We all have oily hands," laughed Reid. "Mine are always pretty much lubricated."

There was a silence. Tallulah could feel her face turning red as she thought about the implications of that statement.

"I mean, with oil," said Reid. "Hand oil. The kind your skin makes. The kind that means you can't touch paintings at the museum. Or most of this lab equipment."

Tallulah had never been much of a flirt, in large part because she didn't want to deal with the consequences. Men usually took flirtatiousness in one of two ways: as an invitation to a pursuit that she generally wasn't interested in, or as evidence that she was a silly girl and not to be taken seriously. And no good had ever come from flirting: her best relationships, with her high school sweetheart Tobin and her exchange-student love Omondi, had grown from deep friendships and shared interests. All of her other entanglements had held some element of disrespect, either for her boundaries or for her intellect.

But Reid was different. He *saw* her.

And as far as she could tell, he liked what he saw.

Screw it. She'd signed herself over, body and soul, to the Ranch for the summer. She was going to flirt.

And screw Rowan's warning. There was no harm in flirting, surely.

"I know that," Tallulah said with a wry smile. "I can't imagine anything else you could possibly have meant."

Reid grinned at her, knowingly, which sent an electric thrill through Tallulah's body. "Let me show you how the incubators work."

The Ranch's dinosaur genetics lab was housed in one of the three wide rectangular buildings that made up what Reid and the other staff called "the Complex". The other two were attached to the omnivore and carnivore nurseries and their massive, many-acred outdoor enclosures; the lab was perpendicular to them both, and had two covered breezeways that connected it to the Omni and Carni buildings, as they'd been dubbed in the age-old tradition of insider nicknames.

The lab itself was windowless and brightly lit, but its sterility was more reassuring than cold. Tallulah had spent plenty of time in labs, after all, and this one was meticulously organized and extraordinarily well-equipped. It was set up as a rectangular galley of sorts. In the middle was a dou-

ble row of workbenches with centrifuges
and various lab equipment on top and stor-
age shelves underneath, punctuated every
fifteen feet or so by an enormous freezer. A
few high-back stools were scattered at the
benches; there was a white lab coat draped
over one. Each side was lined with glassed-
in incubators of varying sizes, from small
breadbox-sized enclosures that would have
fit newborn human babies to enormous
glass cubes taller even than Reid.

Reid touched a sequence of symbols on
a keypad next to one of the large cubes. A
complex circuit-like network of thin lines
glowed a warm red and pulsed for a few
seconds before disappearing again. "Heat's
built right in," Reid said with more than a
hint of pride.

"Did you invent that?"

Reid laughed. "I appreciate your high
opinion of my engineering skills," he said,
"but no, that's outside my skill set. There's
a company in Singapore that developed
this technology for neonatal intensive care

units. I commissioned these from them."

"How did you explain the size to them? Did you just say you had a really, really big baby?"

Reid laughed, a full, rumbling sound. "You're funny, you know," he said. "Humor isn't always common in scientists, but it's very welcome out here. No, I told them it was for my own benign purposes, and offered to make a large enough charitable donation to name the NICU at Mount Elizabeth Hospital after the company if they would leave it at that. So they did."

Tallulah's head spun. "How much did that cost you?"

"Enough." Reid pointed at a medium-sized incubator that contained a leathery oblong egg a little bigger than an ostrich's. "It was worth every penny. Do you see that egg? Which dinosaur do you think it's from?"

"That's a trick question," said Tallulah.

"You can't tell without seeing the embryo."

"That is, indeed, the received wisdom," said Reid with an excitable grin. "And it's true for fossilized eggs. But living dinosaurs, we've found, have eggs as distinct as birds'. Different colors, different shapes, different thicknesses. It's amazing. Here, let me show you."

As he launched into a long explanation of dinosaur egg taxonomy, Reid's face lit up the joy of being in his element, of finding a willing audience for something he adored. This was clearly his special interest. He was, indeed, incredibly knowledgeable, and the information went down even easier since it was delivered in his deep, warm voice.

That voice was like a bear hug, like a massage. She wished she could listen to him speak all day. It rumbled, with a vibration that made her shiver and imagine his mouth on her, his words muffled.

I would kill for a massage from this

man.

Reid talked with his hands when he was teaching her, but his movements were more graceful than forceful. He threw his arms wide to demonstrate the massive variety of structural morphotypes of living dinosaur eggs, and she wanted to run into those arms and hold him. He drew on the workbench with a gloved fingertip to illustrate the dendrospherulitic structures of some fossilized eggs, and she imagined that same finger running down the length of her body, from her lips to between her legs. He cupped his hands together to show her how small a juvenile *Protohadros* was at birth, and she imagined him holding the small creature gently and tenderly, protecting it as if it were a baby.

Reid stopped. "Are you feeling all right?" he asked. "You're looking a little flushed, Tallulah Cole."

"Oh! I'm fine. Don't worry. Just the, uh, heat of the lab coat, I guess," she said quickly, flustered and embarrassed. *Did he pick up on any of that?* "I sometimes over-heat."

"Do you want me to adjust the temperature? There's only so much leeway I have, because of the reagents, but I can bring it down a little bit."

"No, please don't worry! I was just… thinking."

"About dinosaurs, I presume?" Reid gave her a cheeky, friendly grin.

It occurred to Tallulah, suddenly, that Reid wasn't stupid: he must know the effect he had on the people around him, on anyone who was attracted to men. It was like another splash of cold water on her face. *This must be why Rowan told me not to go for him,* she thought. *I wonder how many summer students he's had here? How many he's slept with? And then sent home at the end of the summer, discarded like shards of eggshell?*

And why would she think he'd go for

her, in any case? She was pretty, but hardly runway material. And this man was perfection personified.

Her desire curdled. She was just another kid, she thought miserably. Another summer grad student, here to muck out the dinosaur stalls at a ranch belonging to a superstar scientist who somehow also had enough money to name a wing at a Singaporean hospital, and *also* was legally dead.

"You know what?" said Reid. "Let's get you out of here. Enough dinosaur eggs for today. I'm sorry, I should have thought more carefully. It's been a long day for you."

"Oh, no, please, I am so interested!" cried Tallulah. "I haven't studied them yet in any detail, that's supposed to be part of next year's coursework. Please? I want to know everything."

There was that good-humored grin again. "Thirsty Tallulah," he said. "Thirsty for knowledge. And probably for some water. Or a cocktail, maybe, after dinner."

A little ember of hope flared in her belly. A cocktail. Not a beer with the guys, not a Coke. A cocktail, after dinner.

"I accept," she said with all the subtle flirtatiousness she could muster, "on all three counts."

"That's settled, then. I'll show you all the eggs here, you'll take notes, and then I'll deliver you back to your room for a glass of water and a rest before dinner. We'll eat at my house, all the staff, including you. It's become a tradition for new folks' first full day on the property, though it's been years since we've had anyone new."

Years? "I look forward to it."

"I just have one question," said Reid.

"What's that?"

"What's your signature drink?"

"That is a good question," said Tallulah with a sly smile. "How well-stocked is your bar?"

"Very."

"Well, then," she said. "I love a good old-fashioned. I'm a bit of an old-fashioned girl."

He held out his hand to shake hers. His grip was both strong and gentle, and even through the gloves she could feel the delicious warmth of his skin.

They held the handshake just a moment longer than was necessary. When they let go, Reid brushed the inside of Tallulah's wrist with his index finger, a feather-light touch that made her shiver.

"It's a deal," he said. "An old-fashioned for Tallulah, an old-fashioned yet modern woman."

CHAPTER 8

The sun was sinking low towards the horizon, and the giant leaves of prehistoric trees reached up to meet it. Fluffy clouds, pink-tinged in the early evening light, were scattered like cotton balls across the wide Missouri sky.

Tallulah turned on the bathroom light. She'd chosen one of her only two semi-formal outfits: a fitted, knee-length black halter dress to show off her shoulders, with a thin white sweater stashed in her black leather handbag in case of an evening chill. Black leather platform loafers added two inches of height, though not enough to make her anything other than petite. She went meticulously through the routine she'd always used for evenings out: tinted cream, a hint of shimmer, blush, winged dark-brown eyeliner to bring out the forest depths of her green eyes. Warm red lipstick.

She doubted she'd need blush at dinner with Reid.

She dabbed a tiny bit of gloss onto her lips. Her skin shimmered and her eyes shone. For the first time in a long time, she felt beautiful. Desirable.

It was also the first time in a long time that she'd felt *desire*.

Her heart began to pound again. It had been years since Omondi had gone back home, and the men she'd been with since then had been... unremarkable. Perfectly nice, for the most part, with one or two exceptions that she'd nipped in the bud and blocked on every channel. Nice-looking, with nice jobs, holding nice conversations. They'd gone to restaurants and bars and comedy nights, had a few drinks, chatted about their daily lives and current events. Sometimes they'd gone out again, and then again, for more drinks and dinners and shows. Occasionally they'd bring her home for a nightcap, looking out over the city lights from a sixteenth-floor condo or gazing at uplit trees in the backyard of a townhouse, and she would end up in their bed. White sheets or grey sheets or blue sheets, the masculine scent of beard balm and Old Spice. 90s slow jams or smooth jazz or chillhop. Sometimes, if the mood was right, she could even convince herself for a while that there was something deeper, as they kissed and touched and moaned.

But it never lasted. There was always something empty about it.

Dinosaurs bored most of them, though they listened politely, as one does on a date. Most of them had been looking for a girl who was smart but not too smart, successful but not more successful than they were. Sex with them had been perfectly nice, but there had never been any real passion. It felt performative. At the end of the night, or in the bright light of morning, regardless of how satisfied she was physically, Tallulah had always been a bit sad and wistful. Longing for that deep connection that never came.

Until now.

Until Reid.

The door to the outside squeaked as it opened, and then there was a knock at the bedroom door, startling Tallulah. "It's Rowan. Reid asked me to fetch you. I figured you'd be ten minutes late."

"To fetch me?" Tallulah suppressed a giggle.

"That's what he said."

"Well, I'm here," said Tallulah, opening the bedroom door and sauntering out.

Rowan was wearing a crisp black button-down linen shirt and straight dark jeans, and they'd pulled their salt-and-pepper hair into a stubby ponytail. The look worked.

"How did you know I'd be ten minutes late?" asked Tallulah.

"I took a wild guess." They gave Tallulah a rueful half-smile. "My girlfriend always needs ten minutes, too. Though she always tells me three minutes."

"Your girlfriend? Is she here?"

"Like I said, you're the only woman on property," Rowan said. "Lise is back home in Columbus. I'll see her at the end of the summer."

"How long have you been together?"

Rowan did a bit of mental math. "Fourteen years."

"Wow. And it must be tough, being apart for so long."

"It is," said Rowan. "But it's worth it. I've got my dinos, and I've got my girl. Maybe I don't get to have them both at the same time, but two out of three ain't bad." They gestured to the door. "Our Jeep awaits."

A camo-painted Wrangler sat on the dirt road outside. "Your chariot, madame," Rowan said, bowing. "You've got shot-gun."

"Hop in," called James from the driv-er's seat.

Tallulah hopped in. The Jeep smelled new. James was dressed up, too, in a light-weight blazer and button-down. "Does Reid always have a dinner party when someone joins the staff?" Tallulah asked as Rowan got in behind the passenger seat.

James and Rowan exchanged a glance. "I wouldn't know," James said. "I think you're the first new person here in a while. There hasn't been anyone else hired since I arrived."

"So you're the second-newest?"

"We're all the second-newest," Rowan

said. "We were all hired at the same time. Reid put a full staff into place to run the Ranch. It's been like that since the beginning."

The Jeep gave a mechanical roar as James put it into drive and hit the gas. "So… did you all get a dinner party, then, on your first night?" asked Tallulah in a small voice.

Both of the others laughed. "I guess so," said Rowan. "But not like this."

As they drove along the side of the bowl's downward slope under the darkening sky, Tallulah considered this new information. Reid was hosting a *dinner party* for her. Just for her! With everyone in attendance! It was like a debutante ball. Was Reid so excited to have her there that he wanted to celebrate her in front of everyone? Could it mean she might have a chance with him, perhaps, one day, if she proved herself professionally?

She smoothed the skirt of her dress and twirled a lock of hair around her finger nervously. Reid Canmore. Throwing a dinner party, with all his staff, at his own home, for *her*.

And yet, she couldn't shake the persistent strangeness at the Ranch. Why *had* she fainted when she'd first arrived? It wasn't like her. She'd chalked it up to dehydration, but now she wasn't so sure. They'd confiscated her phone; she was totally cut off from the rest of the world. Reid Canmore was legally dead, but alive and well and astonishingly attractive. And there were, apparently, pens full of carnivorous dinosaurs.

If it was a trap, it was one that seemed perfectly suited to her in particular.

"I'm going to ask a question that will probably sound pretty silly," Tallulah said. "Please humor me, okay?"

Rowan laughed – a bit nervously, it seemed. "Shoot."

"This isn't a cult, is it?"

There were peals of surprised laughter from both James and Rowan. "A cult!" Rowan hooted. "A cult! Honey, do you know how disinclined I am to *ever* get anywhere close to any kind of religion? I did that shit for the first twenty years of my life. Never again. Ever."

"I know this place is pretty weird," James said through his laughter; his voice was soft, but his laugh was loud and high-pitched, almost giggly. It was endearing, like a child's. "But I promise, it's not what you're thinking. You're not about to go to some weird ritual where you're eaten by a *T. rex* while we all chant phrases in ancient Sumerian."

"You know," said Tallulah, "that thought hadn't even crossed my mind. But now that you mention it, so specifically, I'm both reassured and even more worried."

James reached out and gave her a brief, friendly pat on the knee, his other hand on the wheel. "You're good, Tallulah," he said. "You're not in the line of fire here."

"What does that mean?"

"He means that if there's any danger, it's not to you," said Rowan.

"I'm... glad?" Tallulah said. "But..."

"We're almost there," Rowan interrupted. "You'll see it once we crest this hill."

A few seconds later, she did.

A grand house – *a villa,* thought Tallulah – stood at the edge of a copse of those giant-leaf trees. It was a wonderland of brilliance. Little lights were dotted like fireflies among the trees and on strings between them. Lanterns lined a long flagstone path from the road to the front door. A small square pond beside the path was lit from within, a rich blue-green glow.

The house itself was modern, half-hidden by the trees. A central structure of stark white walls bore an enormous window, through which Tallulah could see a floating staircase and a glass chandelier that resembled a fall of rain from the soaring ceiling of the foyer. The rest of the house was stacked artfully and asymmetrically around the structure. Windows abounded; in each one, a beautiful domestic interior scene glowing with warm light.

"It's incredible," Tallulah whispered.

"He tore down the house that was there before and built this one. The old one was falling down. The bricks were all crumbling and one of the columns was cracked through."

Columns? A sickening thought occurred to Tallulah, as she pictured a red-brick colonial house in her mind. "This wasn't a plantation, was it?" she asked timidly. "It wasn't a plantation house?"

"God forbid," spat Rowan, as James pulled the car up at the side of the road and parked it. "I wouldn't be caught dead. Jabez Smith owned a lot of the land near the Missouri River, but this ranch was only ever worked by free people. It was one of the stipulations Reid had when he bought it. No blood at the root."

"Well, then, we're aligned on that," said Tallulah. She opened her door and stepped delicately out of the car and onto the flagstone path.

The front door opened. Reid himself stood in the doorway, a tall and graceful shadow outlined by the light within. He wore dark jeans, a black fitted button-down shirt and an oxblood-red wool jacket that made his shoulders look like they could hold the world.

"Welcome," he called out. "Thanks for driving, James. Tallulah, I'm glad you're here."

Tallulah walked towards him, drawn inexorably, as if by a tractor beam. He turned slightly, as if to listen to someone inside the house, and the golden glow of the closest lantern illuminated his face in profile: the stark line of his jaw, the strength of his nose, the precision of his cheekbone. He was so gorgeous that Tallulah could barely breathe. His beauty was an almost physical presence; she watched every move his body made, hungry for him.

Was this what it was like, being a dinosaur? Helplessly following instinct?

Did they, too, feel this *need?*

Or perhaps this was just her first time falling completely, totally, utterly in love?

The thought seemed absurd to her rational brain. Lust, yes. Limerence, probably. But love? That needed time and space to grow, didn't it?

She turned the thought over and over in her mind as she walked towards Reid, who still stood in the doorway. How could she possibly be in love? She barely knew this man. Until recently, he'd been just a name in a scientific journal – another dead professor, survived only by his work.

She ought to be terrified, not lustful. She ought to be planning her escape. She was a scientist-in-training; it was her job to look at the evidence.

But she was too busy looking at Reid.

He turned his face back towards her, and gave her a broad grin. Her knees nearly collapsed under her. How did he have this power over her?

And now he was holding his arms out towards her to hug her hello. "Tallulah," he said, in his deep velvet voice. "Welcome."

She stepped into his embrace. His arms enfolded her and held her close for a long moment. She breathed in: his scent was intoxicating, woodsmoke and spice and that mystery *something,* deeper and more feral. Tallulah was thunderstruck. She had never, ever felt like this. Reid's warmth, his strength, even the gentle tickle of his breath on her hair – she wished she could bottle this moment. She knew she'd be thinking about it back in her room, in her own bed, wishing he was there, imagining that her hands were his...

And then he let go. "Thank you," she said as he stepped back, her voice no more than a hoarse whisper. "Your home is beautiful."

"Thank you," he said with that same intoxicating grin. "I can't take all the credit; I had a lot of help with the design. But I did want to make sure there were lots of windows, and lots of light. It gets dark out here at night."

"I'm ready for dinner," said Rowan from behind Tallulah. She turned around to see them and James sauntering up towards them. "A person can't live on sandwiches alone."

"Come on in," said Reid, gesturing inside. "There's plenty. Oh, Tallulah, I almost forgot." He reached over to a small table next to the door, and held out a highball glass. "An old-fashioned."

There was, indeed, plenty. Charcuterie boards, set out on long tables in the enormous foyer, were heavy with fruit and jam and pickled vegetables and thinly sliced dry sausage ("Nico worked at a restaurant in Sardinia for a few years before he came here," Rowan told Tallulah, "and he made the sausage himself. We don't ask what's in it. It's just good."). There were bowls of dried fruit and nuts. From down the hall, where Tallulah assumed the kitchen was, there was a sweet-spicy-savoury scent that she couldn't quite place, but was tantalizing nonetheless.

The walls were white, punctuated by huge Rothko-esque abstract paintings that exuded a meditative calm. There were bottles of champagne in scrolled silver buckets at the ends of each table, and bottles of red wine next to them. Tallulah finished her cocktail and then poured herself a glass of red. She took a long sip, and then another. It was remarkably smooth. She wasn't sure she needed liquid courage, per se, but it couldn't hurt.

The room was buzzing with others who Tallulah hadn't yet met. There were about two dozen staff in various states of formal-wear. A hapless-looking and pale young man, piling his plate high with sausage and cheese, looked as if he was wearing his father's suit. An older man with very dark skin and light brown eyes, perfectly turned out in slim black pants and a white shirt, smiled at her and gave her a small wave.

She was, indeed, the only woman.

"Told you," said Rowan from behind her, as if they could read her mind.

"Can I ask you something?" Tallulah asked in a low voice. *I may regret this*, she thought. But the wine had already started its work of disinhibition.

"You can ask," said Rowan. "I can't promise I'll answer."

"Fair enough." Tallulah took a deep breath. "Why did you tell me not to pursue Reid?"

Rowan was silent. Their face was blank – not unfriendly, but closed and impassive. Other staff milled around, their chatter in stark contrast to Rowan's stillness; they looked at Tallulah with friendly curiosity. There was music coming from hidden speakers somewhere, upbeat saxophone-heavy dinner-party jazz. Lights twinkled everywhere. Despite the grandiose size of the foyer, the atmosphere was warm, almost intimate.

Tallulah's anxiety mounted. Had she ruined everything?

After a moment so long it felt like an eternity, Rowan sighed. "Will you trust me if I tell you it's complicated?"

"I'm sure it's complicated. But can you give me the basic outline? Is he married? Is he not interested in women? Is he really mean once you get to know him?"

"Look, Tallulah," Rowan sighed. "I'm not going to make rules for you. You're an adult. I'm giving you my advice, based on what I know and you don't."

"But he's not a secret cheating ass-hole?"

A short, sharp laugh escaped Rowan's throat, loud enough to attract the notice of a few other staff chatting in a group nearby. "No, he's not married and he's not a secret asshole. That's not the problem. Not even slightly."

Tallulah opened her mouth to speak, and then closed it again as she saw Nico walking towards them, a plate in his hand. "Did you try the sausage?" he asked with his gap-toothed grin.

"I did," smiled Tallulah, both relieved and frustrated. "It's delicious."

"Have some more!" Nico shoved the plate, heaped with a variety of sliced meat, between Tallulah and Rowan. They each took a piece.

As she chewed, Tallulah considered the situation. She was frustrated – *so* frustrated – with Rowan's caginess about Reid.

But even her frustration was minor next to the massive relief she felt. Refraining from falling in love with Reid was *advice*, not a rule. It was specifically not a rule! Rowan had said so! And Reid wasn't secretly an asshole. *Not even slightly,* Rowan had said.

So he was single, and kind, and brilliant, and he looked and smelled like *that*. Sure, he lived on a secret ranch in the middle of nowhere; sure, there was some mystique around his background and his legal status as a living person. But all of that could be overcome, surely.

What am I thinking?

"What are you thinking about?" asked Reid's deep voice from behind Tallulah, startling her out of her brief daydream.

"Oh! Um. Dinosaurs?" she stuttered, thrown off guard.

Reid laughed. The sound of it set Tallulah's heart alight. "Right answer," he said. "I knew I brought you into the fold for a

reason. Do you want a tour of the house before dinner?"

"I'd like a tour as well," Rowan said
sharply.

"It's nothing you haven't seen, Rowan,"
said Reid with a smile. "Hasn't changed.
I'll just show Tallulah the sights. If we ar-
en't back in twenty minutes, you have my
permission to send a search party."

"Ha," barked Rowan, a little sourly, as
if Reid had hit a sore spot. "I'll keep that in
mind."

Maybe they used to be together...?
wondered Tallulah. But no, that didn't
make sense; Rowan had mentioned their
long-term girlfriend, and said that Reid
wasn't a cheater or an asshole. It had to be
something else.

Her train of thought was obliterated by
Reid's hand on her arm. It didn't even seem
possible, but she was getting *more* sensitive
to his touch. She craved it. "Let's start in

the greenhouse," he said, gently guiding her towards a small alcove on their left that led to a hallway. "We'll go from there."

Whatever Tallulah had imagined about the interior of the house, the reality was far more beautiful, and far more sophisticated.

The "greenhouse" was a massive, two-storey conservatory, its walls and ceiling of curved glass. It abutted the forest outside, and with the light from inside, Tallulah could see the giant leaves of the miraculous prehistoric trees outside the glass structure, as if standing guard over their indoor family. Plants were everywhere: hanging from the ceiling, on the floor, on wrought-iron stands and shelves and platforms. The floor was made of river-rock, artfully lain in patterns. Tallulah thought she could hear the trickle of a small creek somewhere. "You've got a forest in here," she breathed.

"Of a sort," said Reid. "I know it looks chaotic, but I promise it's very well-organized. I normally keep my lab activities to the lab, and keep the house as a sanctuary for myself, but this is the one exception. I love having the greenhouse here. It's good for the indoor air. And it makes me feel alive." He took a deep breath in through his nose, and exhaled with a smile at Tallulah. "Try it."

She inhaled. The greenhouse smelled fresh like the first day of spring. Reid was right: the scent and the oxygenated air made her feel alive. And he was standing so close to her, his hand still on her arm, that she still smelled his woodsmoke-and-spice scent.

Every nerve in her body stood on end, in anticipation.

She looked up at him. "I feel so alive, too," she said softly. "I feel daring."

He gave her an unreadable look, but didn't take his hand away. "I'd say, Tallulah Cole," he said softly, "that anyone who's willing to throw themselves into something new so quickly and completely has the right to call themselves daring."

He gently guided her towards another door. "Most of the rest of the main floor is just functional. But the back stairway is this way. Would you like to see the upstairs?"

"I would," she breathed. "I would indeed."

The "back stairway" was a much less grand, but no less elegant, set of white marble stairs at the back of the house beyond the kitchen, flanked by simple iron railings. At the top was a door. And through the door was an airy gallery hall with white walls, a wide-plank wooden floor and a curved white roof bisected by a channel of intricately shaped blue glass that twisted and turned like a mighty river. The grand staircase at the front of the house was at the other end of the hall; Tallulah could tell by the very top of the cascading-water chandelier that hung above it.

On the walls, between the five wooden doors, hung paintings of dinosaurs.

"This is astonishing," murmured Tallulah.

"This is my gallery," Reid said proudly.

There must have been dozens of them. Small paintings and large ones, in every style she could imagine. A series of framed pencil sketches of an *Archaeopteryx* made a vertical line down one wall, next to a huge photorealistic portrait of a *Stegosaurus*. On the opposite wall, a Warhol-esque repeating print of a *Hadrosaur* in a rainbow of colors. A marble plinth held a bronze statue of a dinosaur head, so abstract as to be nearly unrecognizable, but if Tallulah squinted, she could just about see how the curves and angles came together. One corner held what looked to be vintage engravings of dinosaur bones along with early, now nearly comical, reconstructions of what the creatures might have looked like.

And directly across from the exit from the stairwell was a painting of two *Apatosaurus*, one smaller than the other, their necks entwined like swans, their bodies pressed against each other…

"Do you like it?" asked Reid.

"Do I like it?" echoed Tallulah. "The gallery? It's unbelievable. Where did you collect all of these?"

"Over the years," he said. "There are more in there. Shall I show you?"

"Of course," said Tallulah in a half-whisper, overwhelmed.

Reid guided her towards a door at the far end of the hall. Behind it was a bedroom, dimly lit by a modern standing lamp: dark linen bedding, a wood-burning fireplace, a single enormous painting of a *Tyrannosaurus rex*.

No. Not a *T. rex*. It had a similar shape, and a similar head, but this dinosaur was larger – it towered over the trees in the painting. Its arms were powerful, not small and vestigial. Its muscles bulged. It was beautiful and terrifying and entirely a mystery. It shouldn't exist.

Reid's body pressed against hers. His muscles, like the dinosaur's, were taut with coiled power.

Tallulah breathed in sharply. Her body, already primed, felt as though it was on fire. Heat rose into her cheeks.

"Oh my God," groaned Reid. "I'm sorry. I didn't even think. This is my bedroom. I got so carried away with the dinos… I didn't mean to make you uncomfortable. I'm so sorry. This is so inappropriate."

"No! Reid! Don't be sorry! I'd love…" She gulped. Was she going to do this? She was. "I'd love to see the paintings. And your bedroom."

She turned towards Reid and looked up at him, into his eyes. His pupils were enormous in the dim light. His lips were slightly parted as if he were about to say something. Or kiss her.

He brought his hand to her face, resting his palm gently on her cheek. "Tallulah," he said faintly. "I –"

There was a crash from downstairs, laughter, and a raucous shout. "Reid!" shouted someone – Rowan? – up the grand staircase. "Everyone's getting so hungry they're smashing their wine glasses!"

Tallulah's face went hotter with embarrassment. "I'm sorry," she said. "I'm the one who's been inappropriate." Her chest hurt with disappointment; her desire foundered.

"No, no, no," said Reid with emphasis. "Listen, Tallulah, you're beautiful. You're fiery. You've got guts. I… look, let's continue this later, okay? There's a lot to do right now." He brushed her hair away from her forehead with a feather-light touch of his fingers. "We'll sort it out. I promise, we'll talk about it later."

"I…"

But he was already on his way down the hallway towards the stairs at the front of the house. "There is no way in hell," he cried, "that anyone here can claim to be hungry."

"Cheese and crackers do not a dinner make," crowed someone else whose voice Tallulah didn't recognize.

A bell rang, summoning everyone to the dining room.

CHAPTER 9

Dinner was served at a long table in an airy modern dining room, bare of decoration with the exception of another water-like chandelier and an enormous painting of a *Tyrannosaurus rex* in full carnivorous roar. It was a blur of conversation, laughter, inoffensive dinner music, inside jokes that went over Tallulah's head, and masterful food.

She heard, saw, tasted almost none of it. Every other sense was dulled. Her whole sensory complex was focused on the man sitting at the head of the table.

"You know why alligators taste like chicken?" asked Nico, sitting across from

Tallulah.

"Why?" she asked.

"Because alligators and chickens share a common ancestor. A dinosaur."

"Well, yes, I'm familiar…"

"Which means," crowed Nico excitedly, "that neither of them tastes like chicken. They both *taste like dinosaur!*"

Tallulah stared down at the half-eaten chicken breast on her plate. The butter-thyme sauce was divine, the meat was tender, and somehow she was no longer hungry.

Chicken, she thought. *I've come a long way from that nickname in the past few days.*

"Don't worry," said another man whose name she didn't know, his brown eyes crinkling at the corners. "Nico doesn't mean any harm. It's like an initiation. You've got to face reality before you can live with it."

A glass clinked rhythmically, loud enough to stop the conversation. The music faded.

"Don't worry, everyone, this is a short announcement," came Reid's booming voice from the head of the table, about ten feet to Tallulah's right. Everyone quieted entirely.

Reid stood. He was already tall, but now he seemed a golden giant in comparison to everyone else at the table. Tallulah could almost see, almost taste the delicious tension between them, like a bright electric river pulling her heart towards him. She was transfixed by the sight of him as she watched his mouth move. His voice filled her.

She couldn't stop thinking about the moment in his bedroom. *You're beautiful*, he'd said. *You're fiery*.

And with his regard, she realized it was true. That, at least to him, she *was* beautiful and fiery.

She was courageous.

She was smart enough to be here.

To have found him.

"As many of you noticed, we have a new hire," Reid said. He gestured at Tallulah, and gave her a small wink and a smile.

All other thoughts ceased. There was no more hesitation or wondering: she *needed* this man. She was utterly and entirely in – love? Lust? Limerence? All three? – with the owner of that smile and those eyes.

Reid Canmore. Who thought she was beautiful.

"Tallulah Cole, would you please stand up?"

Anything for you, she thought.

"Of course!" she said, obeying. Her face was red. She knew it. She couldn't bring herself to care.

"Tallulah is a graduate student in the

Department of Applied Paleontology at the University of Missouri, Columbia. She'll be working on a variety of projects in the lab with us this summer. As you know, we don't take on summer students… well, ever." There was a muted chuckle around the table. "But Tallulah managed to find us, she's smart and very capable, and I think she'll be an excellent fit."

Just go with it, she thought, her face a fiery red.

"Tallulah? Would you like to say a few words?"

"Um…" She looked at Reid's face; his expression was kind, and a bit amused, or perhaps proud. "Sorry, I didn't prepare a speech. Er."

"Speak from the heart, Tallulah!" said Rowan from a little ways down the table - teasing, a little rough, but not cruel. There was some good-natured laughter. The group hadn't turned on her yet.

"I've loved dinosaurs my whole life," said Tallulah. As she spoke, her voice became less hesitant. *You're beautiful*, Reid had said to her. *You've got guts*. "I was obsessed with them as a child. Most kids grew out of it. I didn't. So I decided I wanted to do dinosaurs forever."

"And now you're doing dinosaurs forever," said Rowan good-naturedly.

"For-e-ver," added Nico, showing his missing tooth as he smiled.

"Forever. That's right," said Tallulah, looking directly at Reid. "I love dinosaurs. I'm obsessed with them. I wanted to find somewhere to be surrounded by dinosaurs all the time. To breathe them in. To learn everything there is to know about them. And, as it turns out, I found the person – the people," she corrected herself quickly, "the *people* who want the same thing."

Reid just smiled at her. She radiated desire, hot and bright as the sun.

"And a very unexpected person at the head of all this, but someone I'm glad to know," she said, astonished at her own boldness. "Reid, thank you for letting me be here and for sharing your dinosaurs with me."

Tallulah sat down, her heart pounding so hard she thought she might retch. She'd properly embarrassed herself. She'd put it all out there, and she shouldn't have.

She wanted to sink into the floor – but more than that, she wanted Reid.

She looked back up at him, terrified that she'd ruined everything.

Reid was smiling broadly at her. "I'm flattered and honored," he said.

"I think we're all just glad you're not actually dead," said Rowan, deadpan.

There was a laugh from everyone, and the tension was broken. "That's kind of you," said Reid, "but you're still going to have to clean up those champagne glasses you shattered during cocktail hour."

"Cocktail hour?" hooted Nico.

"Forgive me for trying to class this place up a bit for the lady," Reid said with a smile.

The table descended into chatter and the clattering of utensils. Tallulah's capacity for wild courage had been exhausted. She still couldn't face the chicken, but she speared a piece of broccoli as Nico and James started chatting about the Ranch's need for a new generator. She thought she noticed them stealing a few glances at her... but that would be warranted, wouldn't it? After her little speech?

She'd embarrassed herself. She couldn't decide if she regretted it or not. *I guess we'll see what the result is,* she thought.

Maybe she wasn't out of courage after all.

About ten minutes later, once everyone had eaten their fill, a few staff members got up and started clearing everyone's plates. A few others, yawning, rose and started towards the front door. Reid himself rose and followed them.

"I think that's our cue, Tallulah," said Rowan from down the table. They hadn't spoken much to Tallulah all night, having been deep in conversation with the well-dressed, dark-skinned man who'd waved at her during *cocktail hour*.

Disappointment shot through her. "Already?" she said. "No dessert?"

"We aren't much for sweets, this group," said Rowan. There was a firm edge to their voice. "And we go to bed early." They herded Tallulah out of the dining room and into the grand foyer.

"I don't think that'll be necessary yet," said Reid from behind Tallulah, startling her. "Oh, sorry," he said, noticing her small jump. "Didn't mean to scare you. The others know the way back to their cabins."

"Reid," said Tallulah, firmer this time. "I think it's time for everyone to go."

"I did have a few things to show Tallulah," said Reid. "I'm happy to drive her back."

There was a heavy, tense silence. Rowan frowned. Tallulah's heart soared, and the most sensitive parts of her body swelled. This was it. This was what she wanted.

Wasn't it?

"Tallulah," said Rowan. "What do you want to do?"

She took a deep breath in. "I'd like to see what you wanted to show me," she said.

Rowan shook their head. "This situation has officially gone beyond my pay grade," they said. "Goodnight, Tallulah. I'll see you tomorrow."

"Please don't worry, Rowan," said Reid. "I've taken all the necessary precautions."

"Oh, yes," Rowan said with a tight smile. "I'm sure you know exactly what you're doing."

They turned and strode towards the front door. "James, Nico," they called. "We're leaving. Tallulah has a late-night lab session. Something about pteranodons, I think."

Again, those furtive glances from the two men as they followed Rowan.

And then they were gone.

Tallulah leaned against the appetizer table, trying to seem sultry — but there was a sudden sharp pain in the fleshy heel of her hand, below her thumb. "Ouch!" she cried, pulling her hand away quickly and standing up straight. A crescent-shaped slice dripped bright red blood.

"What happened?!" asked Reid urgently.

"I think Rowan didn't tidy those broken glasses," said Tallulah tightly.

"Steve? Ahmed?" Reid called out towards the kitchen. "Can you please look after the broken glass here? I'm going to take Tallulah to get bandaged up." He took her arm. "There are bandages upstairs. If you'd still like to join me…?"

It was as if the pain of the injury was a pebble on the beach, and her desire for him was a wave breaking onto shore, swallowing it up with the ferocity of her need. "I cannot think of anything I'd like more right now," she breathed.

Reid smiled. It was as if the sun had come out after years of rain. He took her arm, gently. "Shall we?"

Reid's bedroom was a paean to perfect balance. Dark linen bedding with a subtle pattern of lines and crosses; crisp white pillows and a white shearling blanket. The soft and subtle crackling of a low-burning wood fire behind glass. The broad-leafed trees, barely visible shadows through an enormous window that took up most of the far wall.

And above the bed, that huge painting of a dinosaur even more ferocious than a *Tyrannosaurus*.

Tallulah looked more closely at the painting. It was a masterful study. The dinosaur stood on its hind legs, alert and looking directly at the viewer, against a backdrop of trees and little scraps of sky. The rough and nubbled texture of its skin was crafted with the painter's brushstrokes along with light and shadow. Its jaw was mighty, its head held high. Its tail curved around its haunches, coming to a thickly muscled point. Its arms, much larger than a *T. rex*'s, were powerful and regal.

Its eye was blue-green, the pupil a dark oblong void like a cat's, and far more intelligent than Tallulah had ever dreamed possible.

"It's magnificent," she whispered.

"It's a portrait," he said. "Of the first *Tyrannosaurus gloriosa* we ever hatched here."

"The first... what?"

"We've been doing some experiments," Reid said. "DNA research. Figuring out which genes do what – and how we can build a better dinosaur."

The thought was too big for Tallulah to comprehend.

"You got it to... sit for a portrait? Or stand?"

Reid laughed, yet again. "I think I'll keep you around, Tallulah," he said. "You're hilarious. No, it's from a photograph. We don't actually have a death wish here, as much as it may seem so sometimes."

"Well, you're already legally dead."

"Let's get that hand seen to, before it drips more blood on my floor," Reid said. "I'm not a doctor, but I've done a whole lot of field first aid training."

He led her into the ensuite bathroom. Again, Tallulah was amazed. Dark marble floors, an enormous soaker tub, double glass sinks set into a long quartz-topped vanity with dark gold drawer pulls, black river-rock on the floor of the shower. "This will sting a little bit," Reid said, situating her in front of one of the sinks. "But it's necessary."

"I'm not afraid of a bit of pain," said Tallulah.

Reid gave her a crooked grin. "I'll keep that in mind," he said.

Another wave of desire crushed her, brought fire to her cheeks and between her legs. She was *ready* for him. "Do your worst," she half-whispered, in as sultry a voice as she could find within her while her hand bled.

Reid pulled a plush black washcloth from a drawer in the vanity. He wet it with warm water from the sink and a bit of gorgeously fragrant soap. "Here," he said gently, as he took her bleeding hand in his. "Let me see."

He blotted at the blood with the washcloth. Tallulah cried out as it made contact with the cut itself, which had begun to swell. "I know," he said. "Just another moment, and we'll rinse and wrap it."

It *hurt*, Tallulah had to admit. But Reid was so gentle that it barely mattered. His fingers stroked the back of her hand, gently and comfortingly, and she could feel the sheer strength that he was holding back. *He could do anything he wanted to me*, she realized. *Anything.*

The thought nearly made her collapse.

"Are you okay?" Reid asked.

"I'm perfect," said Tallulah quietly. "I mean. I'm happy. Perfectly fine and happy. It hurts a bit but I trust you."

"You trust me?" Reid's eyes danced. "Well, that's certainly nice to hear." He turned the warm water back on again; the *shhhhh* from the tap was soothing. "Rinse now, and then wrap, and then we can focus on other matters."

He guided her hand to the stream of water. It washed away the blood in a rush of dilute pink against the glass. He blotted it dry with another dark washcloth and opened a small package of sterile gauze, pressing it against the injury. Tallulah hissed. "I'm sorry," he said. "Almost done." He wrapped the gauze tight around her hand and wrist, between her thumb and fingers, and kept a steady pressure on the gauze above the cut. "Try to move your fingers and thumb, okay?"

Tallulah did. It hurt, but the movement was easy. "Perfect," he said. "It didn't get your tendons. No permanent harm done."

"Thank you," Tallulah said. "You're an excellent field medic."

"I have my moments," said Reid. He was still holding onto her hand; he began to stroke the inside of her wrist. "Tallulah," he said. "This is a highly unusual situation for me."

"How so?" Tallulah's eyes were wide. "What do you mean?"

She was on a knife's edge. *Please don't turn this down,* she pleaded with him in her mind, but kept her face as expressionless as she could - which was not very. *I need you.*

"Well. First of all, we don't normally have summer interns. We don't normally have anyone else at all. No one has joined us for... years, I think. Not since Rowan and the others."

"I understand. I'm unusual."

"You are, Tallulah," Reid said in a burst. "You are *very* unusual. I've never met anyone like you. You're daring. You're curious. You're beautiful, and you're incredibly strong. Your muscles are..." He paused, breathed, and for the first time, Tallulah understood that he must have been holding back, too. He wanted *her.* "You love dinosaurs — you understand why I love them, too. You're a little obsessed with them, like me."

"I'm a lot obsessed," she said. "Dinosaurs are my life."

"And mine." Reid was emphatic, passionate. His fingers moved up her arm as goosebumps rose on her skin. "They are my life. They are, absolutely, my life. And I've never met a woman I can share that with."

"Well," said Tallulah softly, "now you've met me."

"May I ask you a question?" He moved closer to her. "It's a personal one."

"Of course," she said. "I have no secrets."

Reid paused for a moment as he collected his thoughts, and then looked directly into her eyes.

That was it; this was the big wave, the one that would drown her. She could barely meet his gaze, so strong was the pull, so powerful was the want. She wondered if it was survivable, to want someone this much. Blood rushed again to her cheeks, her nipples, between her legs. She felt dizzy.

"I know this is unconventional," he said quietly. He was so close; she could smell his scent. "And I would never want to be inappropriate with you. I want you to understand that it is *only* a question. It is not a request from your boss, and you are welcome to say no."

"Please, just ask," she whispered.

"Tallulah," he said. "Please trust me that it's taking all of my courage to ask this, but I would be a damn fool if I let this pass me by. If you're willing, and if you feel whatever it is I'm feeling… would you come into the bedroom with me?"

As she stood stunned, he slowly brought her hand to his lips and brushed her wrist with a gentle kiss.

CHAPTER 10

There was no room for conscious thought – or any thought at all, really. Tallulah ached for him with every square inch of skin on her body. Every sensitive place yearned to be kissed.

"I'm sorry," Reid said, misunderstanding her silence. He let go of her hand and looked away.

"No! No, no, please, Reid, of course I want to come into the bedroom." Her words came out in a rush. She reached for his hand with her uninjured one. "I want that so much."

He was so much taller than her, she couldn't reach her face high enough to kiss him. Instead, she brought her lips to the inside of *his* wrist and brushed it with a kiss – and then gave it a small lick.

His skin tasted of salt and woodsmoke and that same mystery *something*: primeval, ancient, captivating.

With a groan, Reid wrapped his arms around her and lifted her off the ground. He carried her easily into the bedroom and laid her gently down onto the soft linen of his bed, and then laid down beside her, his face an inch from hers, his eyes bright. "You're sure you want this?" he asked.

"Reid," Tallulah murmured. "I've wanted this since the moment I met you. I want you so very, very much."

Reid raised one finger to Tallulah's face and traced her cheekbone. It made her shiver, sending bolts of pleasure into the rest of her body. "The feeling is mutual, dinosaur girl," he said, and kissed her.

He tasted glorious. She was hungry for him, thirsty for him; she was starving and he was sustenance, she was parched and he was a great river, overflowing its banks. He moved his mouth to her ear, biting her earlobe just hard enough to elicit a soft yelp. "Just a little pain," he whispered into her ear, his voice rumbling. "It accentuates the pleasure."

Tallulah could barely breathe, let alone speak. She moaned as Reid gently pushed her onto her back and pinned her wrist down, below the bandage, with one hand. "Let's keep this one out of the way, shall we?" he said softly into her ear, before moving down her neck and kissing the place where it met her shoulder, half-covering her with his body.

She moaned again, louder. His muscled body against her, his lips brushing and tickling her neck, the smell and taste and feel of him – she had never wanted anything so much in her life. Her hips thrust forward, almost involuntarily; she was desperate to be touched. Between her legs there was a wetness and a throbbing so hard and deep that she could barely stand it.

And – yes, there was a hardness against her hip, she realized. And it was... sizeable.

"I need you," she breathed. "Please."

"Do you, now?" whispered Reid into her neck. She could picture his smile; the thought only heightened her need. He nibbled at her neck a few more times, and licked her gently as she had licked his wrist.

"Please," she begged, her voice barely audible. "Please, please, Reid, please, I need you to touch me..."

Reid ran his free hand slowly, gently down her body. He circled each breast, trailed his fingers down her stomach until he reached the hem of her dress. Tallulah gasped, parting her legs, anticipating what she prayed was next. But Reid grasped the hem of her dress and pulled it up and over her head, releasing her other wrist momentarily. "You won't be needing this at the moment," he murmured, and then kissed her again.

Tallulah lay on her back, her lace bra barely holding in her nipples, her legs apart. Reid pinned her arm again. With his other hand, he reached between her legs and pulled her underwear down and then off with a single fluid motion. He kissed her as his hand came back to tease her: he touched the insides of her thighs, traced the wetness there.

"Please," she begged.

She felt him smile as he kissed her. "I'll do better than that," he said softly. "Watch me."

He let go of her pinned wrist and kissed her throat, her chest, paused to tongue each nipple as she gasped at the sensation. It felt as though her whole body was on fire, in the most delicious way. Every inch of her skin was primed for Reid's touch. She was a raw nerve, capable only of pleasure.

Tallulah watched as he kissed his way down her body, excruciatingly slowly, still teasing her with one hand. Close, so close to where she wanted him. And then, finally, with one finger, he brushed the bud of flesh that was the center of her desire.

She let out a moan. There was another chuckle from Reid. "Feel good?" he asked.

Tallulah had no words. She knew nothing other than Reid, his scent, his skin, the feeling of his hands and his mouth on her, the knowledge that this gorgeous, brilliant man, this magnetic creature, was here with her, and it had only begun.

"You're spectacular," Reid murmured to her as he kissed her stomach, and lower down. "You are beautiful. Look at you."

And his tongue met the place where she longed to be touched.

All else ceased to exist. There was only Reid. There was only his tongue, lapping at her gently at first, and then more insistently.

It was broad and prehensile; never in her life had Tallulah imagined that it was possible for a tongue to do what his was doing.

Her legs were wide, and she spread them wider still, pressing herself against his mouth, crying out helplessly as his tongue worked on her. He had settled into a gentle rhythm now. It was as if he'd read her mind. He seemed to instinctively *know* what her body wanted in each moment: dipping his tongue inside her, replacing it with a skillful, probing finger as he licked her. The sounds she made, her moans and breaths and involuntary cries of delight, seemed to excite him, too.

Her body was on fire with need. She was nearly senseless. Reid's tongue was relentless. She had no idea how she could possibly withstand this. Was it possible to die of sexual delight?

And then Reid cupped his lips around the center of her pleasure, taking it into his mouth, suckling it gently.

She exploded. There was a starburst of pleasure so intense it was nearly painful, radiating out from the center into the rest of her body. She shuddered uncontrollably, her legs and buttocks clenching. Waves of orgasm nearly pulled her under. There was a gush from inside her; Reid chuckled and lapped it up, happily.

Tallulah couldn't speak. She could barely make a sound. Her breath came in ragged gasps.

"Give me just a moment," he rumbled. "I believe I'm also... overly clothed."

She watched, transfixed and still panting, as Reid unbuttoned his shirt and slipped it off his body. His shoulders were perfect. His belly had a softness to it, but was clearly strong. He pulled off his jeans. His erection strained at the fabric of his boxer-briefs.

Tallulah, red-faced and still nearly insensate, managed a grin. "Is that for me?" she whispered, sultry.

With sudden urgency, Reid tore off his boxer-briefs and returned to the bed, on top of her. He kissed her roughly, probing with his tongue. She tasted herself on him. "Tallulah," he groaned. "You taste magnificent. You are magnificent."

"You," she breathed. "You are the god of desire."

He brought his mouth to her ear again. "I need to be inside," he whispered, his voice deep and resonant. "Is it safe?"

"Yes," she said. "I'm safe. Are you?"

"Yes," he said. "Oh, Tallulah."

He reached down and guided himself into her, groaning as he did. She watched his face as his eyes closed, overcome with his own rapture. She had never seen a more beautiful sight.

They rocked together, senseless with sexual fervor, exulting in each other. Reid pinned both of her arms down over her head and growled low in Tallulah's ear; it was enough to send her into another orgasm, deeper this time, her entire body overtaken by ecstasy.

And then Reid, too, cried out. He gripped her tightly, his body shuddering involuntarily. She could feel a rhythmic gush of thick fluid inside her as his cock spasmed. He held onto her as his orgasm wracked him, as if she were the only thing keeping him tied to reality. Every sound he made, every moan and cry and shuddering breath, was like air to Tallulah. She listened hungrily, kissing him, touching every inch of him she could reach, stroking his arm with a feather-light touch and feeling the goosebumps rise under her fingertips.

They lay together, kissing tenderly and hungrily, as their breath slowed, as they slowly returned to their bodies.

About twenty minutes later, all hell broke loose.

The warm lights in the bedroom went suddenly red. There was a piercing wail from an alarm in the hallway, like a siren turned up to maximum volume. It echoed and ululated for a few seconds, and then a mechanical voice said: "CONTAINMENT BREACH. CONTAINMENT BREACH. REMOVE ALL UNALTERED HUMANS FROM THE AREA IMMEDIATELY."

"*Fuck,*" shouted Reid, more a roar than a word. *Much* more a roar. "What the fuck?!"

"What's going on?" cried Tallulah. She scrambled for her underwear, and realized they'd been flung across the room at some point.

"That's the Carni breach alarm," said Reid urgently. "It's never supposed to go off, because there's never supposed to be a breach. I made sure of it. What the fuck?"

"I don't know," said Tallulah, trying with all her might to keep calm. "We need to get out of here, I think?"

"Come with me." Reid pulled her to her

feet by her good hand, and gave her a quick but gentle kiss. He pulled on his pants, not even bothering with his underwear, and grabbed his shirt. "You have ten seconds to put on your dress, and then we've got to go."

Tallulah found her dress crumpled in a pile by the bed, and threw it on with the speed and grace of a college student who routinely wakes up late for early classes. The underwear was nowhere to be found. *Guess I'm going commando, then.* She slid her feet into her platform loafers. "Ready."

"Impressive." Reid looked down at her, buttoning his shirt up. "You know what? Get up on the bed and hop on my back. It'll be quicker that way."

"Are you sure? I weigh a lot more than you might think."

Reid gave a short laugh. "Tallulah Cole," he said. "You are simultaneously the smartest and most ridiculous woman I have ever met." He gestured to the bed. "Hop up."

He was right: he barely seemed to register the weight of her. With her piggybacking on him, Reid ran in great graceful strides out of the bedroom, down the hall and down the back stairs. Rather than the bright and airy glow of the chandelier, the dinosaur art was bathed in hellish red light that pulsed in time with the alarm. It made Tallulah's head spin.

"The others will be heading off-property already," he said quietly, "but we don't have that option. The safe container isn't far, though. You'll be okay in there."

"What about you?" asked Tallulah. "Won't you be in there with me?"

Reid didn't respond. With her on his back, he ran out the door and into the night.

They fled together through the forest in the dark, branches raking their bodies, until Reid found a narrow path. "You remember this path," he told her breathlessly.

There was a loud, inhuman scream from the deep woods, and a roar.

"*Fuck*," muttered Reid again, and he bounded into the forest in the opposite direction, leaving the path behind.

The darkness was nearly complete, yet somehow Reid was able to avoid smashing into tree trunks or tripping on roots or undergrowth. Tallulah clung to him for dear life, her arms looped around his powerful neck, her injured hand aching. Even as terrified as she was, she wanted to kiss his neck and make him shiver – to flutter her eyelashes at the pulse point at his throat, daring him to grab her and kiss her…

"It's just up here," whispered Reid.

There was a small clearing, ringed by broad-leaf trees, dimly lit by a half-moon that shone through a gap in the tree cover. In the middle of a clearing was a shipping container. The corrugated sides did not shine in the light; they seemed almost to melt into the darkness.

Reid ran to it and touched a spot about halfway down the container, feeling for something. There was another scream from the forest; this time, it trailed and bubbled to nothing. Tallulah knew, in the most primordial part of her, with the instinct of billions of years of evolution, that it was a death scream.

"Got it," growled Reid. He tapped his fingers in a complex pattern, and the side of the shipping container cracked, opening into a door.

Reid set Tallulah down. "Get in," he urged her. She stepped inside, and he followed. The interior was bare, with small fluorescent emergency lights dotted closely together in a line on each side, giving the space a sick, clinical glow.

"Aren't you going to close the door?" asked Tallulah, fear in her voice.

"Listen," Reid said in a low voice, even deeper than his usual timbre. "I have about one minute, sixty seconds, to explain, and then I have to do what needs doing. Can you be okay with that?"

"I think so," whispered Tallulah.

"Here goes," he said to himself, and then, "Tallulah. I'm legally dead because Reid Canmore is dead. The person you're talking to now is a hybrid."

It took at least ten of those seconds before Tallulah could respond. "A hybrid?" she asked, dumbfounded.

"I'm strong because I have *T. gloriosa* DNA," said Reid. "I'm recombinant. Reid died in a plane crash, and they used Reid's body to make me. I'm still Reid, I have all my memories, but I'm also… more."

"That's… not possible?"

"Not as far as anyone knows who isn't at the Ranch," he said. "There are a whole lot of legal, social and financial implications that I don't have time to explain right now. But what it means in an immediate sense is that, if the carnivores get out, I'm the only one who can get them back in. The *T. rex* scarecrow protocol seems to have failed. But they recognize *me*."

"They recognize you? You mean, as a *T. gloriosa*? Those things are here? They're alive now?!"

"They are," he said. "I hatched them before I died. As far as I've been able to tell," he said, "they recognize me as a leader."

"That's…" Tallulah was too stunned to say anything more.

"Impossible, crazy, awful, terrifying, I know," Reid said, his voice full of… grief? "I understand that this is probably the end of whatever is between us. I just couldn't help falling in love with you." He breathed out sharply. "There, I said it. This bizarre *creature* you see before you is in love with you. And I understand if you can't love me back, and that's okay. I just want you to be safe."

Tallulah reached out and gripped his

hand in her good one. She opened her mouth to speak: to tell him that she loved him, that she'd loved him since the moment she saw him. To tell him that she didn't care what his DNA said about him, that he was everything she'd ever wanted. That his being part dinosaur was *appealing* to her.

And then there was a pounding of the earth, a great beast running towards them at top speed, and a roar so loud that it was the only sound in the world.

A claw screeched against the outside of the shipping container. There was a loud *crunch*. Reid, closer to the door, leaped out, leaving Tallulah alone inside.

"Reid!" she screamed.

"Just stay there!" he shouted. "Stay inside!"

There was another screech, and then a rough *thud* as the dinosaur batted the shipping container roughly across the clearing with its huge, muscular tail. Tallulah tumbled to the floor. Her injured hand hit the wall, and she cried out in pain.

An enormous face appeared at the door, peering in at her.

It was the *T. gloriosa* from the painting in Reid's bedroom. Even in the dim fluorescent light, she recognized it by the pattern of light-colored rings around its eyes. Its eye-ridges were dusted with small stiff feather-like protrusions. The eyes themselves were animalistic, but bore a raw intelligence that she'd never seen in any animal before, not even the other dinosaurs.

They peered into hers as the impossibly huge dinosaur cocked its head and opened its mouth.

Up close, the *Tyrannosaur*'s breath was even worse than Tallulah had imagined it could be: a charnel-house blast of decaying meat.

Instinctively she recoiled, scrambling back on hands and knees into the shelter of the shipping container, trying to hide from the monstrous reptile as it pushed its muzzle in through the door. As of yet, it seemed not hungry so much as curious about this tiny female intruder into its domain.

Huddled against the rear metal wall, heart hammering, Tallulah stared out at the glittering eye of the giant saurian as it peered in at her. Maybe if she stayed completely still, it would just go away. If she could only control her terrified trembling…

The creature opened its jaws and bellowed. Inside the container the sound was deafening, obliterating. Tallulah covered her ears and screamed.

Was this how it was going to end? Devoured by a dinosaur? Her mind flashed to the chain of events that had led her to this lethal impasse. She really had put herself in this situation for a man.

But not just any man. Reid.

And worse: given the chance to do it

over, she knew she'd do the same thing.

Her fugue was interrupted by a vertiginous heave as the dinosaur worked its tail underneath the container, tilting it forward.

And then sudden vertigo, as the enraged beast picked up the container with its powerful arms, tilting it further.

Tallulah felt herself begin to slide towards the opening, towards the waiting jaws that would crush her, the sharp yellow teeth that would tear her to pieces.

She didn't even have the breath to let out another shriek.

There was a mighty roar from the ground outside. "STOP!" shouted Reid in a voice that was only half-human, much deeper than she'd ever heard him. He roared again, a series of sounds that seemed almost like... speech?

The dinosaur closed its mouth and looked at Tallulah. It *sniffed*.

It tilted the container some more, so that Tallulah slid closer to its face; she scrabbled and cried out, but could not resist gravity.

It sniffed again, and again. And then it took its head out of the opening and set the container down on the ground, nearly dropping it. Tallulah curled herself into a ball, whimpering, trying to avoid injury.

The carnivorous creature, outside, made a bellowing sound that was almost a question.

"She's mine," Reid shouted, and then roared again at the creature.

Slowly, slowly, the *T. gloriosa* leaned its head down to give Tallulah one more baleful look. It sniffed deeply, as if proving a point, and then roared angrily at Reid.

"You know what happens if you don't go home now," Reid said in that half-human voice. "Go home. Go home now."

The *T. gloriosa* gave a roar that seemed to shake the stars, so loud and terrible it was.

It turned and ran towards its home in the Carni pen.

CHAPTER 11

"**A**re you hurt?" Reid asked urgently as he quickly climbed into the shipping container.

Tallulah was still too stunned to speak. She stood up gingerly, carefully, shell-shocked by the near-death experience. Her ears rang loudly from the dinosaur's parting roar.

Reid crawled over to her and took her into his arms. Tallulah yelped as he touched her injured hand. "That can't feel good," he said, sorrowfully. "I'm so sorry you're hurting."

"I don't think…" Tallulah's voice was barely a whisper. "I don't think anything's broken."

"Can you stand?"

Reid helped her up, effortlessly supporting her as she leaned heavily on him. "I think I can walk," she murmured. "But I liked when you carried me."

Reid burst into laughter, a loud and almost desperate sound, which turned into a choked sob. "Oh, Tallulah," he whispered, holding her tight. "I waited my whole life to find you. Two whole lives. I thought I'd lose you."

"Ouch," said Tallulah.

"Oh!" exclaimed Reid. "What hurts?"

"Everything," said Tallulah. "Except…"

" W h a t ? "

"Except my heart. It's happy."

Reid smiled his sunbeam smile. "Corny, but I'll take it. So you don't mind that I'm a strange mutant?"

"Reid," she said. "I told you I'm obsessed with dinosaurs."

That's true,"

"You are, somehow, a human who's also a dinosaur. You are," she said, pressing her face into his chest, "the most perfect person for me." She breathed in his scent, and realized that the mystery *something*, that primordial smell that captivated the deepest parts of her hindbrain, must be the dinosaur part of him. "You're perfect for me and I love you."

Reid bent down to kiss her. He held her gently, burying one hand in her hair and stroking her arm with the other. And she forgot everything but him.

Back at the building where Tallulah had been staying, there was a note on the table.

Reid,

I quit.

No amount of money is worth this shit. I'm going to build a house by the ocean and live there with my girlfriend and you'll never hear from me again. You've got my NDA. I know they're not usually sufficient, but my understanding is that mine includes such consequences that it will function as it needs to. I hope that settles things.

Goodbye, dino stud. Have fun with Tallulah. She's not bad. Hope you told her about the DNA.

Thanks for everything.

Rowan

"I wish I could say I was surprised," said Reid, folding the note and putting it in his pocket. "Rowan's great. But I think this place was getting to them."

"They really missed their girlfriend,"

said Tallulah.

"I know," he said. "And now I understand that a little bit better." He kissed her.

She looked up at him, starry-eyed. How had she ever existed before him? It was as if she'd discovered a hidden color, or another dimension. The world was so much fuller, so much more vibrant now that she had someone to share it with.

But she still had a few questions.

"Where's everyone else?" she asked.

"They're off-property," Reid said. "They'll be back in two days. I have a house near Sedalia that's reserved for this kind of prison break. Never had to use it until now, though. When they're back, we're going to run through protocols with every single one of them, because that shouldn't have happened. I need to know why it did, and whether it was human error or... something else."

Something else sounded ominous. "And

I want to know why the dinosaur didn't eat me."

Reid gave her a crooked, sexy grin. "I think it's because he smelled me on you."

Ah.

"And, uh, *in* you."

"Ohhhhhh." Despite herself, despite everything that had happened, Tallulah blushed. "They see you as a leader. So they weren't going to go messing with the boss's girl, is that right? And they knew I was the boss's girl because you... marked me with your DNA."

"That's the theory," said Reid. "It's the dynamic I've seen in *T. rex* groups over time, and it seemed to hold with *T. gloriosa*. But I suppose we've just proven it."

"Does that mean I'll be safe from the big guys forever?"

"I still wouldn't go into their enclosure if I were you," Reid said. " Too much risk.

But it's good to know that it's effective."

"Okay. Next question. Why did I faint when I first got here?"

Reid was silent for a long moment. "We have an ultrasonic device that we installed at that checkpoint, to knock out potential visitors so we can… relocate them if there's an issue," he admitted finally. "It doesn't cause damage, don't worry. We just don't want anyone visiting. I think you can probably imagine why."

"What about the Buzzfeed article?"

Reid rolled his eyes in frustration. "We told her over and over that we aren't a tourist destination. We aren't a destination at all. We're a scientific facility that does not allow visitors. We did not consent to be written about. But you know how those content sites are. The fact-checking is… lacking. Anyway, I've been trying to get it scrubbed for years, but Google's cache can be pretty relentless, and it's tough to get anyone on the phone. So that's also why we got the ultrasonic knockout device."

Tallulah, stunned, let out a disbelieving laugh. "You realize that's how I found you, right?"

"You found the Ranch from that *Buzzfeed article*?" It was Reid's turn to be stunned. "You went to page *seven* of Google?"

"How else was I supposed to find it? There's no other mention of the Ranch anywhere."

"I don't know," Reid said. "Rumors? Whispers in the halls at a paleontology conference? A throwaway reference in a scientific journal?"

"Nope," Tallulah grinned. "It's the internet for me. And a kid called Connor."

"Well, then, bless the internet." He kissed her again. "And... wait, you said Connor?"

"Yes. Teenage kid, skinny, told me approximately where to find you."

Reid frowned. "What did he tell you?"

"He told me it was near Norborne, and asked me not to talk about it, or tell anyone else about it. He said it was just one of those things."

Reid squeezed her good hand. "Give me just one moment, okay? Just one second. I promise, I'll be right back."

He went into the kitchen and turned on the overhead fluorescent light; it buzzed with electricity. From the living room, Tallulah heard him open a drawer, and another, until he seemed to have found what he was looking for. There was a beep. "It was the kid," he said, almost inaudibly, in his low, rumbling voice. "It's okay." A pause. "No, I'm not that kind of guy." Pause. "I said no." A longer pause. "Listen to me very carefully," Reid said. "He's a kid. And it worked out in the end. Really well. Shockingly well. I'm not angry. I should be thanking him. Just tell him to keep his mouth shut from now on, please."

Another beep, and a heavy object dropped into a drawer. Reid walked back into the room, rubbing his forehead. "It's handled," he said.

"Dare I ask?"

"You can ask," said Reid. "But I'd prefer you didn't. Just... all's well that ends well."

"That's good enough for me," said Tallulah.

They took one of the Jeeps back to Reid's house. "We need to get some rest," said Reid, "and my bed is a whole lot more comfortable than these ones."

"Just rest?" asked Tallulah teasingly.

"For now, rest," said Reid. "But tomorrow is another day. And I have some ideas about how to start it."

At the house, they walked carefully through the grand foyer, watching out for glass shards, and up the stairs to the gallery hall.

"I have one more question," said Tallulah.

"Anything," said Reid.

"Can I have my phone back so I can call my parents and tell them I'm okay? I miss them." Emotion swelled in Tallulah's chest, so strong it nearly knocked her off her feet. She *missed* her parents. Tears came to her eyes. "I almost got eaten by a dinosaur and I just want to talk to my mom and dad."

"Here's the thing," Reid said after a moment. "They know you're okay. They got that postcard, and we've got... people nearby. I can't let you call them right now, but I promise you'll get to talk to them soon. I know how much they mean to you."

Tallulah was silent.

"Tomorrow, in fact. I'll set it up. I'll get the ultra-secure VPN up and running and you can introduce me to your parents."

"Oh my gosh," Tallulah said in disbelief. "You want to meet my parents already?"

"It would be my honor to talk to the people who raised such a woman as you."

A tearful smile came to Tallulah's face.

"I've waited two lifetimes for you," said Reid. "And I know in my bones, in my soul, in every part of me that this is right. Every part of my two sets of DNA. That you're mine. That I'm yours."

Tallulah put her arms around him and pressed her face against his chest, breathing in that magnificent scent.

"My dad's going to love you," she said, muffled.

"And now," said Reid, "might I suggest that we retire for the evening? It's been a long day, and I suspect that it may be time for bed."

"Time for bed," grinned Tallulah.

"Those are the best words in the world, coming from you."

With ease, and very gently, Reid picked up Tallulah. "Let's tuck you in," he said, his lips brushing the top of her head, making her shiver. He kissed her forehead gently. "My dinosaur queen."

"My dino stud," she breathed, overcome again with desire. It was an endless flame in her body, her need for him: a roaring fire that would never be quenched.

"Perhaps we'll sleep later, then," he whispered in her ear, and carried her into the bedroom, under the painted gaze of the *Tyrannosaurus gloriosa,* most glorious of dinosaurs.

Also by Lola Faust:

Wet Hot Allosaurus Summer
How Stego Got His Groove Back
Triceratops and Bottoms
Tyrannosaurus Sext

Find out more and sign up for free dino-saur romance at *lolafaust.com*

ABOUT THE AUTHOR

From an early age Lola Faust's fantasies and reveries tilted towards the baroque, the unusual, and the eccentric. Though she entertained curious private journals, it wasn't until she entered the Paleontology program at the University of British Columbia that her fantastic and romantic notions concerning dinosaurs took full flight.

While working towards her doctorate, Ms Faust began writing her signature saurian prose. Today she is employed by day at a leading university in her field, but maintains her anonymous and risque personality online.